The
Weeping
Needle

Stories from the Republic of Bharat

Translated by
P Muraleedharan and M Sreenandan

MAHADEVAN THAMPI

Published by Legend Times Group
51 Gower Street, London, WC1E 6HJ
info@legendtimesgroup.co.uk | www.legendpress.co.uk

Contents © Mahadevan Thampi 2025

First Edition

Translated by P Muraleedharan and M Sreenandan

Paperback ISBN: 978-1-918291-95-7

S. MAHADEVAN THAMPI is a renowned media consultant, journalist, short story writer and novelist in Malayalam (an Indian language). He has more than 15 titles to his credit, including novels like *Alakalillaatha Kadal* (*Serene Ocean*), *Jalaparvam* (*The Saga of Water*), *Azadi* (*Freedom*), *Himameghangal* (*Snowy Clouds*) and anthologies of short stories like *Aparaahnangal* (*Afternoons*), *Aakaashangalude Avakaashikal* (*Inheritors of the Skies*) and so on. Many of his works have been translated into English, Tamil, Kannada, Hindi, Sanskrit and even Turkish. Mahadevan Thampi has won numerous awards for his literary contributions to Malayalam, including the Devaswom Board Award, the Madhava Mudra Puraskaram, the SICL Award by the government of Kerala, and the Uroob Award.

P. Muraleedharan, a renowned senior journalist, excels in translating literary works between Malayalam and English, alongside crafting compelling short fiction. Notable translations include works by Vivekananda, Osho Rajnish and Pinky Virani into Malayalam. A recipient of the Kerala State Award for short film production, Muraleedharan has also co-authored a Malayalam feature.

M. Sreenandan is an IT professional with a passion for cinema and fiction that resonates throughout his endeavours. From his roots as a literature graduate to his current expertise as a software testing engineer, Sreenandan is driven to showcase exceptional works in his native language to a global audience.

Stories

dying horizons

"I looked on in horror as the dog bit my father and ran away down the lane, my father's right hand clutched in its jaws. I rushed after it, crossing the byroad and reaching the main road via the country road, but the dog vanished from sight. It was no wild dog, but a ruthless, cunning canine from the countryside..."

As Udayon Kadachan's words trailed off into a stutter, Dr Balakeshavan's mind conjured up the image of his father, Kallan Kadachan, the forest elder, breaking through the police lines. He'd raised the red flag for the first time on the unreachable branch of the tree on the top of Chemmala, even as his right hand was being torn apart.

A cry of pent-up anger and despair escaped from Udayon's lips. "When I came back, my father's left arm, legs and body were being devoured by a pack of jackals. As I approached, they snatched what they could and fled down the alley onto the country road and eventually onto the highway, disappearing from view. Not a single one of them was a wild jackal – just cunning, ruthless creatures from the countryside."

Before Dr Balakeshavan's eyes unfolded the vivid scene of Kallan Kadachan fearlessly climbing the steep slope of Chemmala, AKG clutched in his left hand, his right hand gripping a vine for support, and his big toes curled around it for added safety. It was an unforgettable journey, one that had taken AKG from the hideout in the valley, surrounded by informers and police, to the safety of a shack atop the hills. The cunning jackals were now tearing apart the very limbs that had saved the great comrade.

Udayon felt tired. He covered his face with both hands, sat down on the bare earth and wept.

"At last, two crows flew in from somewhere and perched on the severed head of my father. When I saw their long beaks dipping into my father's eyes, I shut mine tightly. They were not wild crows, but local birds..."

Dr Balakeshavan felt a pang of guilt at the thought of crows eating up the eyes of Kallan Kadachan, who had captured three men, including intelligence operatives, as they tried to gather information on the comrades, helpers and their party classes in the forest areas after climbing Chemmala. He had beheaded them and placed the heads on sharpened bamboo sticks as a warning to others and guarded the comrades throughout the night.

Udayon's anguished lament for his father's brutal end gradually morphed into a haunting dirge, echoing the wild rain that wailed through the forest, accompanied by the rustle of leaves and the whispers of the breeze. Humans, free from debts when they rise from the earth, live off what the trees provide and ultimately return to the soil to nourish the trees as manure. The dirge implored the gods to let this cycle be the way humans repay their debts, and Udayon, in his sorrow, beat his chest with both hands as he sang.

Dr Balakeshavan felt no embarrassment as the dirge rose from his official quarters, potentially heard by his doctor colleagues. Rather, he regarded it as an inevitable form of self-consolation.

For him, the dirge brought profound relief during deeply emotional events, such as the loss of a beloved one. This had been his experience for decades – a realisation that dawned on him during his childhood when he wandered the forests hand in hand with his father.

Keshavaraja, a young prince of the Venad palace who

had been educated in England, had no apparent reason to wander like that. The young man, who was supposed to return from England with a law degree, arrived instead with a 'Communist Manifesto'. He began to spread communism in the country, criticising the freedom struggle and the Congress for lacking passion.

The palace servants, who wielded power through servitude and wealth, did not hesitate to cut off ties with the troublemaker. Believing he would have enough to live on, they granted him eight hundred acres of forest land in Chemmala and a residence in the valley known as Irakkasathram (Inn on the Slope), legally disowning him from the family. When he left the manor, he was accompanied by a sweeper girl named Bhavani, who was pregnant with Dr Balakeshavan. Comrades like EMS, AKG, MN and TV hailed their relationship as a revolutionary marriage.

Keshavaraja was pleased that they got Irakkasathram, a place for leaders to hide and a forest area for conducting party classes. He was also relieved to have the woman he loved. Initially, the couple resided in a section of the inn. It was during this time that Kallan Kadachan, a tribal, became Keshavaraja's best friend. Actually, it was more than friendship – it was a case of blood recognising blood. Kallan Kadachan was the last link in the family line of Kunjhutti, a great woman scholar who had been banished from the Venad palace for an illicit love affair three generations earlier. This perception was reinforced by the fact that his family spoke pure Malayalam without a trace of the local tribal dialect and, unlike the tribals, they were vegetarian. Moreover, people from other tribes called Kadachan a Venadan.

He was the elder overseeing the vast forest area stretching from Oolankuzhi beyond Munnar in the west to Vaga in Tamil Nadu below Kodaikanal in the east. Their camaraderie began when the forest elder, who possessed an extraordinary personality and commanding presence, pointed his sword at Keshavaraja.

When there was no way to provide food not only for his pregnant wife, but also for seventeen comrades hiding in the inn, Keshavaraja ventured into the forest with his woodmen. In Chemmala, the eight hundred acres he owned were dense with trees such as teak, Indian chestnut and wild jack trees. The intention was to sell these for money.

However, as the first strike of the axe hit the base of a black Indian chestnut tree, a bamboo sword touched Keshavaraja's neck. He turned to see Kallan Kadachan, his eyes burning with intensity: "Do not cut down any of these trees. Ask your fellers to return."

Keshavaraja argued, "What, is this fair? I'm cutting down my trees from my land. Why do you want to stop it?"

Kadachan made his case: "Trees belong to no-one – they belong only to the soil. You do not have the right to kill what grows in the soil, thinking that the soil is yours. Will you kill your wife or children just because you own the house?"

The tribal's words took Keshavaraja by surprise. Forgetting the fear induced by the bamboo spear's tip at his neck, he gazed at Kadachan in awe.

"When the trees are alive, they fall down for us to cut when the time is right," Kadachan continued. "In the rainy season, if the logs are dragged into the river, they will flow down by themselves and reach the valley. If you cut down a tree that is yet to complete its life cycle, not yet ripe for work, it will fall onto nine small trees. At least nine thousand saplings will die as they are dragged down through the forest to the valley." He paused.

"Can't you wait until this rainy season? Then the trees you need will fall into the river. They will flow down to the valley without any trouble. Until then, doesn't the young prince of Venadu have the wisdom to wait patiently?"

Keshavaraja had often said that he saw in Kallan Kadachan the Guru he couldn't find even in England. Keshavaraja was fascinated by Kadachan's Forest Code, and the latter, in turn, was impressed by Keshavaraja's communist theories.

The forest produce Kadachan provided to those who came to fell the trees was plentiful – honey, turmeric, traditional medicines. Keshavaraja earned more money from these than he would have from timber, and gradually these became his primary source of income. Kadachan made arrangements for the leaders and Keshavaraja to go into hiding when police harassment and spies became unbearable. Not many people ventured there because they were afraid of the rocks pushed down from the hilltop and the arrows sent their way from Chemmala.

It was during the time when Keshavaraja was forming unions in the tea plantations of Munnar and establishing party cells in the valley villages that Bhavani, Balakeshavan's mother, became seriously ill. After three months of treatment, Dr Hormis, the superintendent of the garden hospital and a prominent evangelist, told Keshavaraja with deep compassion: "Your wife has become dear to God. Cancer is spreading in her, but God will call her back without causing her too much pain. So pray for her to die a painless and peaceful death."

Keshavaraja had a good understanding of his wife's illness. That was why he remained in the vicinity of the hospital, despite the police declaring him a fugitive, accused of killing a policeman in the tea estate.

One night, Keshavaraja carried Bhavani in his arms to Dr Homis's home, knocked on the door and said: "I am indebted to you for all favours you have done for me. However, if she is to have a peaceful death like you say, I have to stay close. This cannot be done here due to many circumstances, so I am going away with her and my son."

Without waiting for his reply, Keshavaraja set off and started to climb Chemmala. Kadachan was waiting on the lower slopes with comrades, ready to flee, but Keshavaraja couldn't see AKG among them – he was still resting in the attic of the inn. Keshavaraja screamed at Kadachan to fetch AKG. Meanwhile, sensing that the comrades were fleeing, the police followed them. Kadachan gave them the slip by taking an adventurous path over the steep slope with AKG in his arms. All these scenes are still vivid for Dr Balakeshavan.

After leading the comrades to the safehouses on Chemmala's top, Kadachan went to the shack – Keshavaraja had a lump in his throat when he described Bhavani's condition. Though a materialist, he prayed to God that his beloved should get a painless, peaceful death.

Kadachan was very upset upon hearing that. But he had a solution. He offered Keshavaraja a divine medicine to fix the time of one's death. He asked when Keshavaraja wanted his wife to pass.

On the top of Chemmala, atop a tall Yama tree, a solitary flower bloomed, turning into a single Yama fruit each year. The fruit, with sixty carpels, symbolised a complete day, like a water clock. Consuming one carpel would bring death after one *Nazhika*[1], two carpels after two *Nazhikas*, and all sixty would lead to death within twelve hours. Death was guaranteed. Later research by Dr Balakeshavan confirmed that revival after consuming the Yama fruit was impossible, as it blocks blood supply to the brain.

The Yama fruit could decide the time of demise not only for humans but also for animals. From tortoises to elephants to wild dogs, creatures would come to Kadachan when they realised they could no longer survive independently. A lion attacked by wolves, with fallen nails and teeth, would seek a swift death; an elephant with a severed trunk couldn't lead a proper life. Yama fruit was their only sanctuary. A tortoise without its shell, a tiger unable to run, a rabbit whose flesh had hardened with age and could no longer forage – all would appear outside Kadachan's watchtower, seeking death. He would

---

1. A traditional Indian unit of time, equal to twenty-four minutes.

administer the Yama fruit as he deemed appropriate, allowing them to choose their end by consuming a specific number of carpels at the appointed time.

All the tribals of Chemmala would have a Yama fruit on their waist bands from the age of eight. At the inevitable moment, they could determine the time of their own deaths, they say.

Dr Balakeshavan recalled with relief that his mother did not have to eat the fruit. Bhavani died peacefully, looking into Keshavaraja's eyes while lying on his lap. Without Bhavani, Keshavaraja was not the same person. He became busy organising party classes as though trying to forget everything else. The insistence that the young Balakeshavan should always be close to him manifested deeply in Keshavaraja like a mental illness during that time. Nothing soothed Keshavaraja except the dirge of the tribals. When the song reached the lowest notes, although the last line of the prayer was a wail with an enigma enclosed, it brought comfort. Keshavaraja spent three years like this before following Bhavani's path. Keshavaraja's death came after Kallan Kadachan placed the heads of those who came to catch the comrades who were hiding in Chemmala and placed them on poles at the approaches. At first, Balakeshavan heard that his father had been killed in an encounter with the police who came stealthily. Some others said that he was felled by people who crept upon him. He also heard that after confiding everything to Dr Hormis, Keshavaraja had decided the time of his death and ate the Yama fruit. Anyway, there were no injury marks on his body. Balakeshavan remembers this even now.

Dr Hormis and his team climbed up the mountain for evangelical duties. They asked Kadachan, "Where is the Raja's son? He is not one to wander the forests; he should be educated and return to help you people."

With Kadachan's permission, Hormis brought Balakeshaven to the city. Kadachchan's son, Udayon, was also taken along. In the city school, Udayon felt suffocated. After two years he returned abruptly, saying that he only needed the forest. Balakeshaven, however, remained.

Dr Hormis gave Balakeshaven the best of education, and Balakeshaven became a doctor. Before leaving for Ireland, Dr Hormis said to Balakeshaven: "Don't forget Chemmala. Even though the forest land you inherited from your father was lost when private forests were vested with the government, it is your ancestral home. Don't forget, your father and mother are there. People like Udayon and Kadachan are your relatives. Likewise, don't go to the valley looking for the inn – it has been encroached upon by an estate in the name of possession. Don't worry that you've lost these assets. You are a doctor. Why do you need other assets? Give what you have in excess of your needs to those who are eligible. But don't you ever forget Chemmala."

Despite the demands of the medical college, Balakeshavan made it a point to visit Chemmala at least once a month. He organised medical camps intermittently, bringing PG medical students with him. During one such camp, a student remarked: "Such healthy people are rare to find! The cadaver for anatomy studies should be from among these people."

Balakeshavan thought that was true. He mentioned it to Kadachan: "The students are demanding the dead bodies of the tribals of Chemmala be made available for study."

Upon hearing this, Kallan Kadachan burst out: "Our bodies belong to the soil that made us, to the trees that raised us."

Ignoring Kallan Kadachan's protests, one student was clever enough to shove a few consent forms (willingness to donate one's dead body to the medical college) into the hands of Udayon's wife. This infuriated Kadachan further.

Balakeshaven tried to calm him: "They are children, don't take it seriously."

Kadachan relented. However in the following three medical camps, he reminded Balakeshaven of the incident, before choosing to let it go.

For the students, a trip to Chemmala was not just an experience of attending a medical camp; it was like going for a feast at the professor's ancestral home. For Dr Balakeshavan, it was not merely a visit as a guest but a pilgrimage itself – a return to his own identity.

But this pilgrimage was interrupted when Balakeshaven received a fellowship, something he had long awaited. When he returned from Canada after two years, he learned about the developments in Chemmala.

The tribals had been completely evicted from Chemmala as part of forest conservation and eco-tourism. Sixty acres of land on a rocky hill outside the forest were acquired to rehabilitate one hundred and twenty tribal families, with each family allocated fifty cents. The official version claimed that the migration was acceptable to the tribals since they were allowed to enter the forest to collect forest produce.

As a doctor, ready to serve always, Dr Balakeshavan had been appointed the superintendent of the medical college, making it impossible for him to be away even for a single day. But when he finally visited the new settlement after learning that Kallan Kadachan had passed away, the situation there broke his heart.

The entire sixty acres allotted to the tribals was rocky, with constructions that looked like soap boxes. People who had lived in vast boundless forests felt suffocated within the confines of fifty cents. Even though the officials had promised them access into Chemmala for collecting forest produce, the authorities hadn't kept their word. The resort owners near the forests encroached on the forest land, with the help of officials, in the name of eco-tourism and trekking. They claimed the presence of forest dwellers may inconvenience tourists. Udayon said that the hands of those involved in illegal timber cutting, wildlife hunting and *ganja* cultivation in the forest were behind the restrictions on the tribals.

Despite trying all they could to bury the body of Kadachan, the rock would not budge. Udayon claimed it did not obey him. Moreover, there was not even a single tree under which they could bury a body as per tradition. Those who tried to enter the forest to bury the body were chased away by the resort lobby and government officials. Finally, the corpse was placed on a rock and covered with soil collected from a by-road nearby.

Udayon, who had burst into tears as he said this, was now sniffling with pent-up anger as he recounted the fate that had befallen his father's corpse, which was devoured by dogs, jackals and crows. He also said: "We were invited to Muthanga and Chengara to participate in the struggle for the lands for which the tribals have rights. Isn't the forest land our mother? Will anyone fight to reclaim her? It was said the struggle was for agricultural land. Why do we, who do not know how to cultivate, need farmland? We need the forest. We are the forest's owners, and the forest is our home. We cannot live anywhere else but there."

When Udayon said again that it was suffocating to stay outside the forest, Balakeshavan told him: "Udayon, I don't have words to console you. But get up, let's find a way to avoid this kind of predicament again. I'm not going to the hospital today."

When Dr Balakeshaven met the department secretary with Udayon and explained the situation, the official, though a close friend, expressed helplessness. "The land issue of tribals is a policy matter of the government. We get the orders, we execute them."

When asked if there was anything he could personally do to help, he made it clear: "Forest laws are strict, and I have no powers to relax them." He paused and added, "We shouldn't forget the expanding tourism. Should we lose revenue worth millions of dollars for a few tribals?"

Were the lives of Kadachan, Udayon and others like them, who protected the forest and wild animals like their own lives, of no value? If it were not for them, would this forest cover, though much depleted, have survived at all?

Balakeshavan was very careful not to let the questions within him spill out. Instead, he gently inquired, "Who can help them with this problem?"

After a moment's thought, the official suggested, "You could try to see the minister..."

The minister, who gave Balakeshavan special consideration for being the son of comrade Kesavaraja, was chronically ill. Balakeshavan thought the minister might show gratitude for the traditional treatment he had once received, which was why he took Udayon along.

"Come, Doctor," said the minister inviting me in. He pointed to Udayon and asked mockingly, "Is this a preparation for a performance of tribal art?"

I covered up my anger behind a very humble smile and explained the situation to the minister.

"Has the doctor also started political activism like your father? Don't you know that times have changed? Which role are you playing? The opposition or the activist?"

The minister's expression changed swiftly from anger to gentleness. He continued,

"Doctor, the land issue of tribals is a political problem. We resolved it only recently. Meanwhile, why are people like you doing this for them—"

Before the minister could finish, Dr Balakeshavan interjected: "I am also one of them."

On hearing that, the minister rose from his seat. He touched Balakeshavan on the shoulder, took him to a corner of the chamber and whispered in his ear.

"These are terrorists. If allowed back in the forest, they will give a base for the revolutionaries and disrupt the peace of our country. Besides, the possibilities of tourism, including trekking in the forest, will vanish."

How could this snivelling minister talk like that about those who had given their lives to protect the revolutionaries in forest hideouts years ago, only to now enjoy the fruits of their sacrifices? The doctor somehow suppressed the anger that surged within him and remained silent.

The minister, perhaps in a bid to pacify him and Udayon, winked and said: "I will look into your grievance, only because the doctor came to speak about it."

His next words were like a polite dismissal. "Are you not leaving? I have a planters conference to attend."

Leaving the minister's office in deep disappointment, thoughts of his father and Kadachan, who had sacrificed their lives for an ideal, flashed through Dr Balakeshavan's mind.

Udayon followed the doctor in complete silence like a shadow. It was then that an idea struck Balakeshavan – to visit an idealistic journalist who could inform the world about the dire situation of the tribals in Chemmala, thus creating a public opinion that the government could not ignore.

When the doctor presented the facts in the presence of Udayon to the journalist, he responded despairingly: "What can I do? I wrote a similar story, analysed it threadbare and filed it. The management dropped it saying that the resort lobby who provide massive advertising to our organisation wouldn't like it. Still, I tried to get this story published in some other media out of compassion for the tribals and because it is an issue that the country needs to know about. The same problem occurred." He paused as though resigned to reality. "What can we do? Today there is no-one willing to stand for an ideal if it means losing revenue." After a long silence, he burst out: "I continue like this because there is no other way to earn my livelihood.. Doctor, sometimes I feel like making lots of money by printing fake notes or smuggling, just so I can start a newspaper or a channel to tom-tom the truth. Without waiting for an answer, the journalist went back to his room.

Returning to his quarters without saying goodbye to his good friend, Dr Balakeshavan's mind was troubled. Why did his father fight, abandoning all his good fortune? For what were the sacrifices of many like his father? For what did Kallan Kadachan, the forest elder, endure all those adventures?

Dr Balakeshavan, kept asking himself these questions and finally conducted a self-examination: "Have you made any sacrifices for anyone in this life?" he asked himself.

Before finding an answer, Dr Balakeshavan went to speak with Udayon Kadachan. "Udayon," he said. "I have never saved any money in my life. After taking what I need to live, I give everything else to hospital patients and others. I might have money in my provident fund – if not, I can get a loan from a bank. With that money, I will buy you a plot with soil and trees. You can die in peace, assured that you will be buried under a tree."

Udayon laughed. "What I want is the forest... the forest soil... Can you buy that for me?"

Dr Balakeshavan had no reply.

A strange silence fell between them. Udayon broke it.

"I know. You can't," he said. "But I have found another way."

Dr Balakeshavan inquired eagerly, "What is it?"

"No. I won't reveal it now. I will tell you when the time is right."

The doctor did not insist further, and they fell once more into silence. Finally Udayon said: "I came to see you because you told me to come, and that you would find a solution to our problems. Now I have to go home, where my wife and children are waiting for me."

Without replying, Balakeshavan took Udayon to the bus station and sat him on the bus which would take him to the rocky hill where his home now stood. Balakeshavan took out all the money from his pocket and offered it to Udayon, but Udayon refused, saying he had more than enough money even after accounting for the bus fare.

As the bus moved, Balakeshavan asked: "It has been a useless journey, hasn't it, Udayon?"

"But I met you! What's more useful than that?"

Udayon said something else, but before Dr Balakeshavan could comprehend it fully, the bus had moved far away.

The doctor could not sleep that night. His mind was full of memories of the forests in Chemmala, where he had wandered as a child. There, under a flame tree, his parents slept. Where was Kallan Kadachan who had arranged for their eternal sleep in the soil of Chemmala?

The doctor pondered those thoughts until well into the morning. Even at dawn, he didn't rise nor head to the hospital. Finally, when the intercom kept ringing incessantly, he hurriedly got ready and went to work.

He did not know how the day passed as he was among the patients and absorbed in the problems of the hospital all day.

When he returned to his quarters that night, his mind was full of the disappointment of a loser. Dr Balakeshavan took tranquilisers and waited for sleep, filled with an unknown sense of anxiety and guilt.

He must have fallen asleep sometime during the night, for he woke up to the continuous ringing of the calling bell. He did not have private practice at his quarters. If it was from the hospital, they would call him on the intercom. So, who could be visiting so early in the morning?

The doctor opened the door anxiously, still groggy from

sleep, to find the chief security officer of the Medical College Hospital standing out the front.

After greeting the doctor, he informed him: "Doctor, I came in person because you didn't pick up the phone."

"What's the problem?"

"There is an agitation."

"Where?"

"At the outer gate of our fourth block."

"Isn't that the morgue? Who are the protesters? What is their demand?"

The officer explained: "In front of the mortuary, a tribal family is observing a protest fast. After hearing what they say, I can't make out what the demand is."

Without waiting for the doctor's reply, he continued: "Without force, I don't think they can be moved. Since they are tribals, use of force could lead to big commotion. I came here to ask what we should do."

Suddenly a thought flashed in his brain. Could it be Udayon and his family? Why did they come there to protest? Could it be that they were at the wrong place?

Without further thought, Dr Balakeshavan went with the security officer to the entrance of the mortuary. There he saw Udayon, his wife and two children sitting in front of the mortuary, surrounded by security guards.

"What is this? When did you come? Why didn't you come to my quarters? Why are you here?"

Udayon and his family did not stand up in respect as they usually would, nor did they reply.

When the doctor repeated the question, Udayon said: "Thought that everything should be made easy so that no-one is bothered. If it is at home, the police would have to come – they need to investigate and file a case. After that, the bodies have to be brought here on a rented vehicle. If it is like this, none of that is needed."

Taking a bundle of paper from his wife's hand and holding it out to the doctor, he continued: "These are the same papers your young doctors gave us when they came to Chemmala. There are fingerprints on the consent forms."

Balakeshavan looked at them. Yes, they were the signed papers for donating their dead bodies to the medical college.

Udayon said without any change in expression: "If it is there, dogs will tear you apart. Here, we shouldn't be scared of that."

Dr Balakeshavan couldn't bear to hear any more. He took Udayon's hands and said: "What are you saying? Get up – let's go to my quarters."

Udayon did not get up. He announced with a wild grin:

"All four of us have eaten the Yama fruit. We have eaten according to a fixed time schedule. We won't even complete another *vinazhika*[2]."

The doctor stood stunned, and all four fell to the floor with their eyes closed. Even then, Udayon's lips were whispering in a terrible trance: "Dogs will not tear apart our legs and bodies, and the eyes of our head will not be gouged out by crows..."

His voice soon took on the tune of the dirge.

"I saw it – a dog with the severed right hand of my dad in its mouth... then the jackals sharing his left arm, legs and body between them... The local crows lowering their beaks into the eyes of the severed head..."

The lines of the dirge suddenly reached a crescendo.

"No. Now I don't see it. I see the sky. Chemmala in the sky... Under the fig tree there are four deep pits... graves. The soil from the skies covers us up... the roots of the fig tree come down into us fast..."

The tone of dirge gradually faded.

Hoping for a touch of consolation, Dr Balakeshavan searched for the solution to the enigma in the last stanza of the prayer – but then the chant unexpectedly stopped.

---

2. A traditional Indian unit of time, equal to twenty-four seconds.

the confessional

The black mosquito with white stripes and spots sat on the step above the sliding panel of the confessional and stared at Dr John Koshy.

The doctor had seen this mosquito before, at the base of the cemetery cross. It circled his head as he whispered into the ear of the priest who had come to administer the last sacrament: "Father, I want to confess immediately after the burial." The priest had allowed him to come to the church for the purpose.

After the burial, the doctor had been shocked to find the mosquito following him with a persistent hum. The Bible says the transformation of His creation would shock the creator. That which gave birth and that which was born shall live. The mission of creation will be fulfilled in many forms and in many ways. Whatever is destroyed will be reborn. No seed in any form is wasted. They bear fruits or pods, or even evolve into dust over time. Whatever is sown will be reaped in one form or the other.

Dr John Koshi saw only one ear – a willing listener to all he had to confess – when the sliding panel sounded to announce the presence of the priest outside the confession booth. He began, pouring out his story in a steady flow.

"Father, I left the country before you arrived in this parish. So I have to tell you a little about myself. I am the son of Kumbanattu Nirappel Koshy Vaidyan. I hail from a family that practised traditional medicine. My father wanted a modern doctor in our family; that was why he ensured I was taught medicine despite our terrible poverty. He sacrificed everything to educate me, hoping I would bring fame and fortune to our family. But when I became an M.D. in microbiology and started teaching at a medical college with a modest salary, he was deeply disappointed. My father's advice was simple: if I couldn't make money through private practice, I should marry a nurse employed abroad and move there. I obeyed.

"I married Elizabeth Kurien, *née* Lisie, a nurse working in Switzerland, and we settled there. Soon I secured a position at the virology centre. Initially, my assignments were in African countries – a paradise for viruses. Though the two-week research trips each month were gruelling, they enriched my knowledge. This African exile was one of the reasons I later became recognised as an outstanding virologist. Life was safe – two incomes, a nice house, a beautiful environment.

"After three years, we decided to have a baby. But when Lisie didn't conceive after two more years, we underwent tests. The results shattered us. Lisie had uterine abnormalities and couldn't conceive. Worse, her heart muscles were severely damaged. We clung to hope, seeking expert treatments that consumed all our savings. Lisie's condition required her to stop working, and her treatments were not covered by insurance. My salary alone wasn't enough. We borrowed heavily. To repay our debts, I began offering private consultations in remote African villages without informing my employer. These assignments in areas lacking even basic infrastructure were gruelling, but I had no choice.

"Despite sharing my struggles with my family, they showed little concern. What mattered most to my father was that I wasn't sending him money – his disappointment stemmed from that. During one call, he expressed his anguish: 'I sold everything to make you a doctor. I thought you would support your younger siblings. But what happened? People like you should build three or four bungalows here, buy estates and

cars for their parents, marry off their sisters. What about you?'
I hung up the phone, I couldn't take it anymore.

"It didn't take long for those moments of discomfort to
turn into bliss. 'Congratulations, John Koshy,' said Sylvia
Davidson, my friend and gynaecologist who spilled the good
news. Lisie was pregnant. Against all odds, the test results
were positive.

"Those were the moments when I forgot myself. I didn't
know how I reached the gynaecology centre. Sylvia cautioned
me as I stood embracing Lisie, that the pregnancy was more
due to God's grace than a medical miracle, and that we
should be careful. Lisie needed rest until delivery and should
be moved to a gynaecology centre. I was ready to sacrifice
everything for my child in her womb. I wondered: what legacy
can we leave behind, other than this link, – our children – that
moves on to the next generation, which is eternal?

"Sylvia shared her concerns with me about the staggering
medical expenses. Ironically, despite my exhaustion, I felt
an unexpected surge of energy. Driven by the need for extra
income, I took on small private consultancies outside of my
regular job. Fortunately, my connection to the virology centre
created opportunities for these consultancies, which came
with rewarding benefits.

"That's when I made my first mistake. Our institution's
head, Dr Ludovic Klosto, a French national with a taste
for luxury, was surprisingly generous. When I requested
his assistance, he included me in a project team. As a
virologist, my role seemed straightforward: fulfil the
team's needs and ask no questions. The promised reward
was staggering – three million dollars. The project, funded
by a multinational pharmaceutical company, claimed to
be developing sanitation projects in Nigerian villages.
Unbeknownst to me, its true purpose was sinister. Under
the guise of disinfection and sanitation, I was tasked with
spreading viruses that would rapidly spread deadly diseases.
It wasn't until I returned from the mission that I discovered

the pharmaceutical company had already supplied drugs to temporarily cure the diseases caused by these viruses. As the virology centre received global acclaim for its timely intervention, a more ominous reality went unnoticed. A sister company, International Oil Corporation, had secured mining rights and marketing contracts for four Nigerian oil fields, granted by the government to fund the drugs, treatment and rehabilitation efforts.

"I felt guilty and angry at this fraud against the innocent. But all of that was forgotten when Lisie gave birth to our baby girl. I named my daughter Rosa, whose tiny feet were like rose petals. When I saw her, when I was near her, when I touched her, I would go into a state of pure ecstasy. It was then that I realised there was nothing I loved more.

"It was not because I was rich with a fortune of three million dollars that I did not go to the virology centre. I wanted to watch Rosa all the time. Rosa, my Rosa. I didn't want anything else when she snuggled close to my heart.

"After I completed my first mission successfully, the head of my institution unexpectedly sought me out. He proposed that I retain my position as senior consultant and continue projects abroad. But the images of infected people seeking refuge in Nigerian relief camps, which I had seen in the papers, flashed before my eyes. They haunted me, leaving an indelible mark on my mind. I decided to decline the offer. But Lisie, unaware of the truth, whispered in my ear: 'No matter how hostile our surroundings, can we survive without working? Don't we need money for my treatment? We have a daughter, shouldn't we provide for her future? Don't we have to be respected in our native place? Don't you need to stand up straight in front of your father?' "Lisie unwittingly prodded me forward, oblivious to the true nature of the projects I was being persuaded to undertake. She did not realise that the cloak of science was being used to conceal atrocities against humanity. Her words continued to urge me on, a painful reminder of the moral dilemma I faced.

"A commentary on the Holy Bible cautions that every motivation, be it good or evil, will ultimately achieve its objective. It warns us to resist succumbing to forbidden temptations, even when they come from those we love. Yet, I faltered, surrendering to the very thing I knew was wrong.

"I went to Somalia and Bangladesh, later to Indonesia and Vietnam with similar missions. For my mission in Lebanon, I risked my life. By then, I had become a millionaire. My efforts were recognised internationally, earning me numerous awards. The world perceived me as a philanthropist, selflessly aiding the underprivileged in challenging environments. However, the truth remained hidden: every mission was orchestrated by those who had deployed me.

"I built a new house in Liat, Switzerland, in the middle of a garden with rare roses without thorns. In the middle of those rose flowers of the same colour, my Rosamol bloomed like another flower, and Lisie was her shadow. At home, my father bought up land wherever he could and transformed the family manor into a palace fit for kings. I helped all my siblings, gave money to all the churches as dad suggested and gave lavish donations to all voluntary organisations for social work. Maybe because of that, whenever I returned home, people found reasons to arrange welcomes and felicitations for me, eager to make me happy. I didn't understand that those days of happiness were the precursor to a huge tragedy.

"On 3rd January 2006, three people came into my chamber in the virology lab: Dr Ruth Davis, our deputy chief and a renowned scientist; Ben Franklin, our security chief; and Derick Geller, the enigmatic owner of MediCorp, a pharmaceutical chain based in Zurich. Ruth explained that Derick had a private project in mind.

"Before speaking any further, Ruth closed my chamber-door from within and lit the red lamp. I panicked a little, and seeing this, the beautiful Ruth said, "Don't you worry, I closed the door so that no-one else could enter." She was like that. At times, she would come in, close the room like this and say that it was great to savour Indian cuisine once in a while. She would go crazy and take off all her clothes and then deep dive into the invisible whirlpools of lust with me. Even though she would often take the lead, it was my mysterious private pleasure. But when she closed the door that day, it made me uneasy.

"Without hesitation, she said: "Dr John Koshy, I want you to lead a project in Kerala, India – Operation Togaviridae. You'll receive a substantial reward: five million dollars." Her words hung in the air, laden with an unsettling anticipation.

"I was stunned when I heard 'Togaviridae'. My research expertise lay squarely within this viral family, specifically on the chikungunya virus. I was intimately familiar with its devastating consequences. Chikungunya, transmitted by the Aedes aegypti mosquito, was first identified in Tanzania in 1953. It was in Tanzania that I conducted most of my research on this virus. The same mosquito species also spreads dengue fever.

"I am considered to be among the leading voices on Aedes aegypti mosquitoes and the diseases they spread. Our research team accurately found the biting pattern of this black mosquito with white stripes and spots – the bites occuring during morning and dusk hours. At one time, the female mosquitoes can lay between 200 and 300 eggs in fresh water. These mosquitoes are capable of flying significant distances, typically ranging from 100 to 300 metres, and up to one kilometre with favourable wind conditions. Our research in Tanzania, which tracked the mosquito's trajectory, speed and distance, garnered worldwide attention.

"Once infected, the mosquito carries the virus for life. If the virus enters a person's bloodstream through a bite, symptoms appear within three days – sudden fever, muscle aches, joint pain and swelling. The initial fever subsides after a few days, followed by severe recurrence of fever that can last up to a week, causing irreversible damage to the body. In some cases, brain swelling may also occur.

"We found that the mosquito eggs can remain intact for up to a year, even in the absence of water. Because the virus remains within the eggs, the hatched mosquito will also carry the disease, perpetuating the cycle of infection.

"Ruth outlined the sinister plan behind 'Operation Togaviridae': to deliberately spread chikungunya and dengue fever in Kerala. She emphasised that, as a native, I would face no obstacles in executing the programme with the aid of voluntary organisations. But I was horrified. I immediately rejected the proposal.

"This is my homeland," I said firmly. "I will not be a party to spreading disease here. If you attempt to carry out this heinous plan through others, I will do everything in my power to stop you. You will be brought to justice and face the consequences of your criminal actions.

"My response, instead of deterring them, seemed to fuel their enthusiasm. Ben let out a sarcastic laugh, inserted a CD into his laptop, and said, 'Take a look at this. We have evidence of the atrocities you committed in Nigeria, Somalia, Bangladesh, Indonesia and Vietnam, along with records of the substantial rewards you received.' He paused, his expression menacing. 'These are trials that would take a lifetime to get completed, and even then, justice might not be served.'

"Ruth chimed in, her voice dripping with malice. 'Why bother with a trial? Suppose this information gets out. Won't the public bay for Dr John Koshy's blood?'

"I was devastated. The secrets I thought were mine had become ammunition for others to use against me. As I sat there drained, Ruth approached me and inserted her own pen drive into the laptop. A map of Kerala flickered to life. She pointed to the red markings on it and explained like a teacher: 'This is Walayar in Palakkad district, let's start here. Then we'll move on to Pathanamthitta, Kottayam, Alappuzha,

Ernakulam, Kollam and Thiruvananthapuram. This is the first phase.'

"I couldn't stand it. 'I can't,' I wailed, feeling helpless. Only then did Derrick intervene. He took out a picture of my daughter Rosa from his overcoat pocket and spoke in a deceptively gentle voice: 'It's so much fun to peel off rose petals one by one!' I trembled with fear, envisioning my beloved daughter's limbs being brutally chopped off. 'I don't need this work, I'll leave the country,' I managed to stammer. Derrick's response sent chills down my spine. He said, 'I don't need Interpol's help to find someone, no matter where they hide. My people will always find them.' He locked eyes with me, his voice dropping to a menacing whisper. 'And, Doctor, you should know that my people are already close to you... watching your wealthy old father.'

"I was rendered speechless after that. When I felt like I was defeated, I gave it one last try. 'Would it be okay if I were to do this in another country or state?' Derrick had an answer for that too: "Not at all, nowhere else in the third world will you find people as health-conscious as in Kerala. If this disease spreads, I can sell drugs worth ₹9,000 crore in just six months. The drug is already manufactured at my plants in India. The only thing left is for you to get to work.'

"I asked, almost in desperation, 'Is there a cure for chikungunya?' Derrick's answer was succinct and chilling: 'Who will know it is chikungunya at first? An unknown illness like a fever? The local doctors will prescribe medications for fever and related diseases. When chikungunya is finally confirmed, they'll go for preventive medicines for other diseases. You need not worry about all that...' Then Derrick spoke as though sharing a joke: 'You have stored mosquito eggs that can survive for a year – that's brilliant! Ruth also has a big collection. If hers goes missing during our journey, you'll have to use yours, won't you?'

"The trap was set, and I had no escape. Derrick's voice grew more persuasive, sensing my surrender. He said, 'This ₹9,000 crore deal is just the beginning. Even if chikungunya fades, related diseases are sure to follow. Medicine will be needed to treat them also. Since chikungunya tends to recur every other season, the demand for our medicine will be consistent. Moreover, sixty percent of those infected will suffer from related illnesses for the rest of their lives, ensuring a steady stream of customers. We manufacture those medicines as well, making this a business with limitless potential. And, as your partner, I assure you that you'll be compensated accordingly.'

"With that, Derrick pushed a leather bag full of money toward me, his eyes glinting with a mixture of greed and triumph. 'Allow me to say, since the doctor is now a partner in this business, that it's a business within a business. We have an order from a group renowned for their versatility and global competitiveness. At the same time, we're protecting the interest of another group that wants to deter foreign tourists and industrialists from investing in Kerala. Will anyone come to an epidemic-ravaged place?'He added, 'If this disease spreads, all attention will be on its containment. Your state's development will be disrupted. Think of the working days lost, the people impoverished by illness. A government that loses control will be despised by its citizens.'

"Derek then paused and reminded me with perfect manners. 'This is a business with three layers. This is not just about financial gains, but also about friendship with countries like Pakistan and espionage agencies like the ISI. We can't afford to miss this opportunity. If you betray us, the rose petals will fly...'

"They bade me goodbye very respectfully. I was trapped in a situation where I cannot confide even in my wife. I knew my wife would be devastated by the depths of my entanglement in this sinister plot. My mind sought refuge in the Holy Bible, but the words offered little comfort. I felt that turning back was no longer possible. I could only keep fleeing, knowing that sooner or later, all paths must come to an end.

"When I revealed that I was heading home with an 'unexpected project', Lisie and Rosa were adamant about joining me. I had to dissuade them, citing the unfavourable climate and Rosa's fragile immunity. Lisie eventually relented, and I managed to pacify Rosa as well.

"Upon arriving in my native state, I initiated the 'sanitation programs' for mosquito control in several districts. I started in Walayar, then expanded to Cherthala in Alappuzha and Pathanamthitta, with the support of local voluntary organisations. As the initiative gained momentum, schools and religious institutions joined in, allowing us to extend our reach to Ernakulam, Kottayam, Alappuzha, Kollam and Thiruvananthapuram. The knowledge that the materials distributed for mosquito control contained the virus carrying eggs of the Aedes mosquito made me terribly upset.

"I sent my parents to the safety of our plantation in Mysore, knowing it would take a month for the mosquitoes to multiply and spread the disease. To protect myself, I took elaborate precautions. Drawing from my experience of living in Switzerland, I adopted a peculiar attire – socks, long pants, full-sleeved shirts and gloves – claiming I had a severe sun allergy. My mantra was simple: avoid mosquito bites at all costs. I retreated to a mosquito-proof, air-conditioned room, where I rested and slept, shielded from the impending epidemic.

"Within a month, the first symptoms began to manifest in localised areas. Patients complaining of fever and other illnesses started flooding the hospitals. Before long, private and government hospitals in southern Kerala were overwhelmed, struggling to cope with the sheer influx of patients. As hospitals overflowed, many patients were forced to return home, left to stand in crowded corridors without even a place to sit. Yet, paradoxically, there was no shortage of medicines. The sudden availability of these medications sparked no curiosity – no-one questioned who had procured them, how they had arrived, or whose foresight had ensured their timely distribution.

"It wasn't until millions had fallen ill and hundreds had lost their lives that the truth finally emerged: the culprit behind the epidemic was chikungunya, a disease spread by mosquitoes that struck during the daytime. I couldn't help but feel a pang of pity for the people who futilely burned mosquito repellent sticks at night, inhaling the toxic fumes in a misguided attempt to ward off the Aedes mosquitoes that struck during the day. My contempt for the government's inept response was equally strong, as they wasted resources on fumigating road dust to kill mosquitoes that actually bred in freshwater sources around homes. As a supposedly enlightened expert, freshly returned from abroad, I felt a searing sense of self-loathing for joining the farce and participating as a volunteer in these misguided efforts.

"Throughout this charade, Ruth maintained daily contact with me. She seemed to talk only about official matters on the phone, but every word carried a hidden meaning. I could tell from Ruth's conversations that Derrick was happy with the situation unfolding in Kerala. Quoting a newspaper report, she asked me why the official figures for the infected showed only 250,000 infected while the actual figure was closer to seven million people. Then she whimpered in a strange voice and said: 'The situation in your state is so pathetic! We are deputing you there with full pay. And one more thing – don't let what happened in your southern districts repeat in the north.' She raised her voice so that someone else could hear: 'When you return, an honour for exemplary services will be waiting for you. Don't forget Rosa.'

"That meant, I had to spread the disease to the northern districts of Kerala, for which I would be handsomely rewarded upon my return. There was also a veiled threat that Rosa's life would be in danger if I didn't do what I was told.

"I went to the northern districts of Kerala. I was in the interior of Wayanad for three days. When I reached Kalpetta on the fourth day, my mobile rang unexpectedly. 'Dad, happy birthday,' came the voice of my Rosa. It was my birthday – I had forgotten. Rosa's voice came through the phone again, filled with excitement. 'I've come to surprise you, Papa! Mummy's here too. We've been at your house in Kumbanadu for two days. Can you come soon?' I was too drained to respond, my mind reeling with dread.

"In the midst of a raging epidemic, my vulnerable daughter had walked right into the heart of danger. Her weak immunity made her a sitting duck. And she'd been exposed for two whole days. The thought sent a chill down my spine. Lisie, oblivious to the risks, might not have taken necessary precautions. Exhaustion and anxiety threatened to overwhelm me. Without even asking Rosa why they'd come, I started the car, my heart racing with a sense of urgency.

"When I reached home, I stepped into the front yard. Rosa's carefree laughter filled the air, her eyes sparkling with wonder. Lisie stood beside her, a picture of serenity. But my heart sank, consumed by a toxic mix of anger, despair, and fear. My reaction was foreign to Rosa, who had never seen me like this before. Lisie, too, was taken aback by my strange demeanour.

"Before I could utter a word, my gaze scanned their bodies, and I trembled. Red blotches marred Rosa's face and Lisie's – unmistakable mosquito bites. I knew the ominous implications. The disease that had ravaged the land had now reached my loved ones. Science, once my trusted ally, seemed powerless against this scourge. In desperation, I sought solace in the Holy Bible – *not a single seed goes waste; in the course of time, it may even transform into dust; whatever may be, what is sown would be reaped in one form or the other.*

"Rosa had a fever on the third day. I went to the best available hospital, but there wasn't even space in the general wards. I met a doctor I knew, and he offered to prescribe medicines for my daughter and advised us to go home. When I told him that she needed to have in-hospital care, he suggested that I should try another hospital. There was no scope in the big hospitals. I looked for average hospitals where even verandas had been converted into makeshift wards to accommodate chikungunya-dengue patients. In the government hospitals, it was difficult to even enter the premises. Patients lay even at the hospital gates. Amidst all this chaos, Lisie also developed a temperature.

"With hospital admissions impossible, we made a desperate visit to a doctor's residence, which was similarly crowded. When I revealed my identity and shared Rosa's compromised immune system and Lisie's heart condition, the doctor's demeanour changed. He discreetly ushered aside the other patients and conducted a meticulous examination of Rosa and Lisie.

"'There's no doubt they both have fever,' he confirmed, his expression grave. 'The symptoms strongly suggest chikungunya... which, as you know, has spread rampantly throughout the region." The doctor paused, collecting his thoughts before speaking. "Rest is paramount for this disease. I'll provide a prescription, but I must advise you that hospitalisation is out of the question. The facilities are overwhelmed, with no beds, rooms or even floor space available. Take the medication and ensure they rest at home.' As he handed me the prescription, he leaned in, his voice taking on a more serious tone. 'You know the risks, given Rosa's compromised immunity and Lisie's heart condition. We must be vigilant for potential complications.'"I navigated through the crowded streets, eventually stopping the car in front of a medical store. The scene was chaotic, with people swarming the entrance. After what felt like an eternity, I managed to push my way to the counter and hand the chemist the prescription. As though anticipating the prescription note with me, he handed me the medicines in a jiffy. What foresight, what immaculate planning!

"Though the fever subsided in two days, on the third day both of them developed high fever and red marks on their bodies. I decided to get them admitted to a medical college for expert treatment. I leveraged all my influence to secure an admission.

"Following an intervention from the Health Department, a section of a doctor's consulting room was made ready for Rosa and Lisie. Despite limited amenities, they received the best possible care and treatment. I struggled to focus on my prayers, pleading with God to prevent Rosa and Lisie's condition from deteriorating further and to shield them from contracting new diseases within the hospital's walls. But the medical college's devastating sights and sounds pierced my heart, shattering my concentration and making it impossible to pray.

"The hospital was a world of its own, filled with unspeakable suffering. Since I was close to the consulting room, I could see everything. An elderly man, unable to stand without support, begged the doctor to end his life, consumed by unbearable pain. An elderly woman, confined to a wheelchair, cried out in agony, her joints aflame. Her anguish seared my very soul. A middle-aged woman admitted she hadn't been able to use the toilet for a week due to her immobile knees and waist. I felt disgusted and helpless. I couldn't help but sob.

"Despite my best efforts to shut everything out, the pitiful hospital scenes haunted me and robbed me of peace of mind. I knew a young man, who complained that he could not drive an auto-rickshaw because his fingers and toes couldn't be bent. He begged the doctor, screaming, 'Please straighten these, doctor.' I knew his anguish and despair was not just about his own suffering.

"A little girl, delirious with fever, murmured on her father's shoulder, 'Teacher, I can't write... my fingers won't bend." Her cry still echoes in my mind. I saw many others too: a child who hadn't opened her eyes in three days, an old man admitted for severe dehydration as he vomited everything he ate, a middle-aged man who wept that he just wanted to sleep. I saw them all in the early days of our hospital stay.

"The days that followed brought countless firsthand accounts of tragedy and despair. I heard of a taxi driver, the sole breadwinner for his family of three children and a wife, who succumbed to chikungunya. In desperation, his entire family took their own lives, leaving no survivors. Another young man, who had sold everything to secure a visa to work in the Gulf, was sent back due to his chikungunya diagnosis. In utter hopelessness, he took poison right in front of the hospital.

"As I watched my daughter and wife receive treatment and care, I couldn't shake the thought of the thousands who were denied even the most basic necessities. The weight of knowing that I had brought this suffering upon them initially filled me with anguish. However, as time passed, the relentless barrage of tragedies numbed me, leaving me feeling empty and desensitised. I was very vigilant about Rosa and Lisie even in this hopeless chaos. Chikungunya had unleashed its full fury upon them. Yet, I held on to hope, drawing strength from the Bible's promise that deliverance is near. I stood guard, watching over them in that hospital for a year and a half.

"My Rosa developed a brain swelling which continued to worsen. I lost count of the number of times she underwent head surgery. My child, who was once like a rose petal, now lay like a lifeless leaf. I could not bear to see her unable to recognise anyone. Lisie, too, suffered terribly, plagued by insomnia and inflammation of the heart muscle – all cruel manifestations of chikungunya's wrath. I could not see her suffering terribly despite every possible treatment. One day the doctors revealed the extent of their helplessness.

"I told the doctors, 'I have the money to make available any expert treatment.' The answer shattered me: 'If she is moved from the bed, anything may happen...'"

"As usual, I sought refuge in the Bible: *a time to sow,*

a time to grow, a time to reap and enjoy its fruits. Father, I became the seed, the crop and the fruit. One day, I even became the bread and wine to the mosquitoes. Taking off all my protective clothing in the veranda of the Medical College Hospital, I became the leftover bread, as they drank only the wine – like the offspring, who did not partake of the bread and wine together like his disciples. Isn't the soil the source of bread? And should the soil not turn back to the soil? That, Father, is what you added to the soil a little while ago...

"But let me ask you one more thing that is not in the Bible: will the confession of the dead be heard?"

Suddenly, from beyond the sliding panel of the confessional box, the priest's ear jerked away and two wide staring eyes appeared in its place. Before those eyes was a huge mosquito filling the confession box. With horror, the priest saw that the mosquito bore the face of the man who had been cremated that morning.

fading moon

"I want to spend a full day with you. Will you please do that for me?"

When Kannur 'boy' Sahali asked this over the phone, James Joseph – the founder and southern zone captain of Magic Lamp, a voluntary organisation which fulfils people's last wishes – was stunned.

He had heard many strange last wishes from those on their death beds, and had fulfilled most of them. But this wish was a first time in the history of his organisation.

An orphaned old woman with fast-spreading mouth cancer had only one wish: she wanted to chew a delightful pan. She had the habit of chewing pan even when she was asleep; she attempted to smile at the sight of tender betel leaves, *arecanut*, tobacco and slaked lime – it was a sight to behold.

Likewise, a girl afflicted with leukaemia, admitted to the children's ward of the cancer centre, asked for a red frock with yellow rose flowers sewn in. He managed to arrange for it just in time. The girl clasped the hand of death wearing that frock.

The last wish of an old beggar, who hadn't even been able to drink a drop of water for a week, was for a sumptuous dinner.

During the brief period that he volunteered for Magic Lamp, he had also come across last wishes which could not be fulfilled at all. A fisherman whose both legs were amputated due to diabetes complications said he wanted to pedal a cycle he had been using for thirty years before slipping into a diabetic coma. An athlete whose spinal cord was cut in an accident wanted to play football with Zidane when death called. He also saw a mother who wanted to see her daughter who ran away from home at the age of ten, fainting into death without her wish being fulfilled.

All those wishes were very relevant. But this last wish seemed very mysterious for James. Why should the boy want to meet a person who had no connection to his life? Why should he think of spending a day with that person?

It was due to these doubts that he asked Dr Balu, the vice-captain of the Kannur zone of Magic Lamp and a doctor in the government hospital there, for details. Balu told him the child was the grandson of Arackal Ahmadunni. Ahmadunni's son was a leather merchant in Singapore – he died in an accident there. When his grandson was afflicted with a disease, he returned home. When it was confirmed that the child admitted in the medical centre in Kozhikode was nearing his death, he decided that his end should come in happy surroundings and hence brought the child home. Balu spoke to that child in person and was convinced of the sincerity of his last wish. Maybe, that was why Dr Balu insisted he go.

"Whatever the case, come over. It is Friday today. Since Saturday and Sunday are holidays, you can stay here tonight and return tomorrow if you start the journey today."

James didn't think much after that and said yes to Balu.

Father Gomez had told him that he should not delay things about near-death people. So he started out immediately. He got a comfortable berth on the train, thinking he would reach Kannur early in the morning.

For James Joseph, the words of Father Gomez were irrevocable commands; he had to obey him. Thirty-five years ago, Father Gomez had found a child abandoned in the crib at the Thangassery Church and he raised him, thinking that he was the son of God. He named him James Joseph and gave him a good education, seeing him become a computer engineer with an MBA degree.

When sending him away for a job, Father Gomez reminded him: "Remember that your past is behind you. You're a new person now. Only come back if you absolutely must, or the scars of your orphanhood will linger forever."

Though he could understand the good intentions of the priest, a lump stuck in James's throat. "Father, I don't have anybody other than you and the people here."

His reply was very serious – it boomed like a revelation in his ears. "Think that no-one is a stranger, and you will have everyone."

Saying goodbye to him, the priest said, "Now it's time for you to build a life with a partner and start a family." He paused, gazing into the distance, and added, "He has already set things in motion for you. That will also happen sooner."

This turned out to be a real prophecy. James was in the fourth month of his job with the Kochi unit of a renowned IT company when it happened – he was on an official trip to the head office in Bengaluru. He got the first train.

When the train reached Thrissur, a girl entered the coach and sat opposite him. The second he saw her, James Joseph felt *here is your partner: the woman got created for you.* Later, she told him she also had felt the same; the moment she saw him, she realised, *I was born for this man here, he is the man God selected for me.*

She was Sujamol for her mother, Sujakutti for relatives and neighbours and Suja Menon for her fashion designer colleagues and friends. Before embarking on her journey to Bengaluru from Thrissur, she was all these personas, but in the next twenty-two hours, she would be transformed into Suja James.

James realised as they sat in opposite berths in the train, speaking like long-time acquaintances, they were discussing not only the future but also the secrets of their past lives. It was then that he saw the angry expression on Colonel KSR Menon's face and the determination in Suja's eyes.

"I only have the right to decide on who I should marry, not my dad. I have already accepted James Joseph as my husband."

These words of Suja cut the relation of blood between them. The colonel minced no words. He said,

"From now on, I don't have a daughter. My daughter Suja Menon is dead."

Father Gomez who helped them get a transfer to Bengaluru, marry and settle there, blessed them to have a great married life.

"You love, and you will be loved."

But to whom exactly was the blessing meant?

For a year, James's life with Suja was heavenly. Seeing them very happy, their friends were envious. Suja's life was completely dedicated to James and vice versa.

But it didn't take long for the flowers of envy to wither away.

It was the vaunted breeze from the fashion world in California that changed everything. Three fashion designers were headhunted from India, and Suja was one of them. When they offered her a huge salary and the infinite possibilities, including acceptance in the world of celebrities, she told James: "I will go and will return to take you with me once I settle there."

"No, no. Don't you go! We are getting more than enough money here, okay?"

That was the beginning of the rift. It grew into weeks of long debates and quarrel. At one stage, Suja asked him: "James, are you envious of me? Does my career growth make you feel inferior?"

That question from Suja was more than James could handle. However hard he tried, he couldn't control himself. The tip of his tongue quivered involuntarily.

"You will say this. I should expect this and more from a woman who denounced the parents who raised her for twenty-two years for a person who she knew for just twenty-two hours. Not just career growth – there will be many more Jameses. Maybe people smarter than James."

Her only reply was: "Let's part ways."

Even months of separation couldn't make any change in her stand. The time gap only made her more adamant.

On knowing that the preparations for her journey to the US were complete, Father Gomez reached Bengaluru and tried to placate her.

"Man shouldn't separate what God has joined," he said.

But her stand was uncompromising. "There was nothing godly here, dear Father. This is only my mistake. The children must pay for what they did to make their parents sad, isn't that so? This is my fault, my big mistake – my separation."

She added one more thing: "Since I have paid the price and endured this separation, I don't have to see my parents again. Also, I cannot re-enter a place where they declared me dead when I am alive..."

And with that, she left.

When James was alone, he felt as though his insides were burning with frustration. That frustration slowly turned into hatred and anger – anger at everything and nothing, for no apparent reason. Father Gomez sensed this and advised him:

"Shed your hatred, and your mind will regain calm."

The priest suggested for him the first path towards healing – returning to his hometown from Bengaluru, where he could escape the memories of Suja that surrounded him.

James got the transfer to Kochi very fast. Afraid that memories would haunt him if he chose to live alone, Father Gomez arranged for him to stay as a paying guest at a home in Marad.

James worked a five-day week, Monday to Friday, 8:00 a.m. to 6:00 p.m. There was no way to while away the time after office hours, especially on Saturdays and Sundays when he had nothing to occupy himself with. When he was alone, memories of Suja drove him mad. He was not interested in having friends or travelling. The priest had told him not to go to Thangassery to meet him. Then what could he do? Father Gomez advised him to go for some higher studies in his spare time. James tried this, but found he couldn't focus.

Seeing this, the priest asked:

"Will you consider another relationship?"

That was the first time James opposed the priest.

"Impossible, dear Father. If you say I should die, I will do that this instant. But not this."

"Then do one thing – you go to the US and meet her. Give her a call at least!"

Though he himself had thought of it many times and dropped the idea, James accepted the priest's suggestion reluctantly. First, he would call her, and then go to meet her in person.

It took great effort to get Suja's number. But in their first conversation, she blocked his advances. The words she used were cruel:

"I am not interested in spending even a second with you. Never call me again," she said. "I don't have the habit of taking back what I have abandoned."

James was destroyed.

Father Gomez advised him that it was best to forget her for the time being. But James couldn't forget her – the memories wouldn't die. The priest's next suggestion was to get himself engaged completely in something else so that the memories wouldn't haunt him. He showed James an easy way to achieve this – in his free time, he should go to hospitals, orphanages or old age homes, where he could help those in need of care. His words were like the word of God to James:

"Be ready to help others, and you too will be helped."

The light in those words showed James the way forward.

It was through his regular contact with people facing imminent death that James began to understand. All the patients abandoned by doctors after their prognoses, and all the old people who heard the footsteps of death louder by the day, would remember their beloved desires that could not be fulfilled until then, in their last moments. When the moment of death approached, they yearned for the fulfilment of their last wish. They were quite sane in those hours.

When they realised in the last few hours before they died that separation from life on earth was inevitable and imminent, and that a return to it was unthinkable and impossible, they frantically looked for loved ones or the things they liked best; or they became anxious about the things they couldn't accomplish and entrusted it to others; or else, a longing that we may consider silly but was very important to them came out in their last words.

Once, an old woman at her deathbed in a medical college hospital, suddenly became cheerful. Blinking her eyes, she looked around and said to no-one: "Offer a sacrifice for me at the temple." It is not known whether her last wish was fulfilled with proper rituals.

On another occasion, a dying beggar while being picked up from the roadside to take him to the hospital, demanded plainly: "Bury me in the cemetery of the little church. Put the twenty thousand rupees in my cloth bag in my grave."

On yet another occasion, a dying woman's last wish was to see her husband, who left her behind after she fell ill. The young woman kept Death away until she met him. She passed away holding his hand.

Due to such busyness every day, James did not have time to call Father Gomez. When the priest called, James apprised him of everything. Once he finished, the priest would bless him:

"Always be merciful and considerate. You too will be treated with mercy."

Once the father asked him: "Should the light of your goodness be confined to a single place? Shouldn't it spread to other places as well?"

The priest was suggesting something James was already

thinking of – a state-wide voluntary organisation to fulfil the last wishes of the orphans who were about to die.

When he realised that it needed large-scale preparations and facilities, it was decided to start on a small scale at the district level. James appointed himself as the captain in Kochi. Nasser was in Kollam and Francis at Kottayam. There were kind-hearted volunteers in every district. Everything fell into place quickly.

It was Father Gomez who named the organisation 'Magic Lamp', wishing that it could fulfil all the wishes of the near-death people like Aladdin's lamp. When the outfit made a website and explained its plans, several people came forward to help it realise the wishes of the orphans in their deathbeds. Thus, the dedicated services of those volunteers were seen with respect and seriousness by the doctors and hospital staff all over.

Sahali's request, and this trip, were the latest proof for that.

The doctor had called the Kozhikode representative of Magic Lamp to the side of Sahali, whose death was believed to be imminent. The doctor requested him to fulfil one last wish for the boy.

"The moment I meet the kid, I should ask him why he wanted to spend a day with the founder of the Magic Lamp," James Joseph decided, as he drifted off to sleep on the train.

In the morning, he realised that he had reached Kannur when Balu woke him up. On the way to Arackal, Balu kept talking about the boy.

"If one sees him, he won't get a feeling that the kid is ill," he said. "A naughty, handsome boy."

Ahmadunni was waiting at the threshold of the Arakkal bungalow. He welcomed them warmly. Beyond the porch, Sahali was swinging lazily on the swing-cot in the open courtyard in the middle of the building. A cute boy – just as Balu had said.

James felt an instant connection with the boy, transcending his present birth. Sahali's special feature was the eyes that spoke without making conscious effort. His uninhibitedness was very unique. There was fearlessness and firm resolve in all his movements. When he clasped James's hands and said hello, the child looked at him intently – a gaze that pierced his soul.

"You know me?" James asked slowly.

"Yeah." The boy's answer was firm.

"How come?"

"I saw you on the site. Then my mother told me. *Uppa* also informed me." He spoke without letting go of James's hands.

When James tried to say something more, Ahmadunni led him aside.

"You have all the time in the world to talk and spend time together," Ahmadunni said. "But before that, let's have a private talk." He paused and continued: "What I'm talking about may seem irrelevant to you, but you have to listen to me patiently. That is necessary to give comfort to Sahali. Please don't interrupt me."

He seemed to have something serious in his mind – perhaps about the child's illness. Or maybe about finding new ways to cure his disease. James notices that on hearing that their talk was about something private, Dr Balu stayed away.

Ahmadunni took James to the outhouse, and, in the middle of a sumptuous breakfast, he began to explain:

"I am a leather merchant. After the death of my wife, my only interest was in making money. I had made lots of wealth in Singapore. But my son was not fortunate enough to enjoy the riches. My son and his newly wed wife had gone for their honeymoon when an accident occurred on the expressway. His new sports car was crushed like a soap box. The bodies of him and his wife were taken out with great difficulty.

"Though a spendthrift and a person who lived his life on his own terms, he was still my son. Without him, I couldn't live in that land. I was about to return home when everything turned topsy-turvy.

"A Malayali girl approached me, seeking a portion of my residence for rent. She had just secured a job and had a child with her – he was one and a half years old. On seeing me, he ran toward me waving his hands. When he was a child, my son Sahali was also like that. I took the boy in my hands and he looked at me and smiled just like Sahali did when he was little. I felt as though I had got my son back.

"For the woman who sought a portion of my home for rent, I gave my residence in full, and I lived there like a paying guest. I listened to her whole story. Her eyes told me she was telling me the truth.

"She didn't have to appoint a servant to look after the child, since she became my daughter. I was his *Uppa* and then, his *ayah*. He had a name, but I called him Sahali, and that soon that became his name – my relatives and the people here think that Sahali is my grandchild."

Ahmadunni took a deep breath and then continued:

"Sahali grew up, and I enrolled him in an international school. On the first day of his fifth-grade examinations, his principal called me and asked me to rush to the health centre. I was frantic with worry and found him lying on the hospital bed, limp and lifeless, like a withered plant in the scorching sun. I was aghast. Myself and his mother, who came rushing in when informed of the incident, spent three days in the hospital with him. He became conscious only on the fourth day.

"The Chinese doctor who treated him comforted us by saying, 'the withered plant has been watered back to life.' He explained that Sahali's condition was a rare and terrible disease, where even with sufficient food, blood glucose levels could plummet unexpectedly, leading to hypoglycaemia, coma and eventually death. The symptoms began with profuse sweating from head to toe, followed by tired limbs and eventual unconsciousness. While elderly diabetics who take insulin regularly might experience this rarely, it was almost unheard of in children. The condition could recur, and research was ongoing at the Diabetes Centre in Sydney and the Pancreas Foundation in California. The doctor suggested we take Sahali to one of these centres to explore possible treatments.

"So, we took Sahali to Sydney and California, staying there for months with him at a time. He underwent numerous medicine trials. However, the doctors ultimately concluded that since Sahali's condition was so new, treatment protocols were still being developed.

"Whenever Sahali's symptoms recurred, we'd hospitalise him, and once he'd recovered, we'd return home. However, we couldn't keep him in school or his mother in the office. How long could we survive in a foreign land? Eventually, we decided to return to our homeland.

"She had nowhere else to go. Since she had become my daughter and he my grandchild, I brought them to this Arackal manor. Here also, he collapsed three or four times, and we took him to the hospital. On each occasion, Providence intervened to save him. Any moment, he could slip into unconsciousness, followed by coma and certain death. If he had a final wish, I was the only one who could help him…"

Ahmadunni, who generally seemed very composed, could not complete his sentence and sobbed. James Joseph couldn't suppress his curiosity.

"You didn't tell me everything. Who is this kid's dad? The family of that woman – her parents?"

Ahamadunni's reply shook James to the core.

"It's you. She is Suja. Your Suja."

James Joseph stood as if struck by lightning. Even during the numbness of that shock, James Joseph felt Ahamadunni's words ringing in his ears.

"She learnt that your child was growing in her womb only when she reached America post the separation. What hurt her most was the way you cast her away saying that she ditched her parents who brought her up till she was twenty-two years for a person who knew her only for twenty-two hours. Otherwise, she wouldn't have left you. After reaching America, all her life was meant only for your child in her womb. Later, she got a transfer to Singapore on learning that it was better than America to rear her child. But..."

Though his words got stuck somewhere for a while, they began booming in his mind with renewed vigour.

"She stumbled upon your website when she was looking for avenues for the treatment and palliative care for her child. She showed him your picture and told him that you are his father. You know, he is a small kid. From then on, his only wish was to meet his dad and spend at least a single day with him. Suja told him at the outset that they shouldn't disturb anyone – you know, that is her nature. But when she was told that the death of her son was imminent, I reached out to Suja's father and informed him of the tragedy, defying her wishes. What he said shocked me beyond words. He said his daughter was dead. I didn't inform Suja of this. You may also say now that Suja James had killed herself. But at least you have the organisational commitment to fulfil the last wish of that child, right? I called you here with that faith..."

When Ahamadunni stopped to catch breath, James Joseph took his hands and begged him as though something snapped within him.

"Oh no, please stop. Don't speak any further."

When Ahamadunni seemed to have calmed down, James asked him: "Can I go to my son? Where is my Suja?"

"She will be with your son... I told her to keep away as I didn't know how she would react on seeing you..."

On hearing this, James Joseph left the outhouse and ran to the drawing room, crossing the corridor to reach the swing-cot in the courtyard. Suja was standing with her eyes closed, both hands her son's shoulders. James couldn't hold himself any longer. Tears flowed like a stream in spate, threatening to drown Suja and her son.

But Suja tried to keep away from James. He was beside himself and spoke between sobs:

"Dear Suja, how much have you suffered?" Then he complained: "You didn't even inform me that we have a son."

She shut her eyes a little more tightly on hearing that. Her lips moved mechanically, "When he was old enough to enquire about his dad, he did so, and I showed him."

James looked at her face. Her eyes were closed.

"Suja," he began in a low voice. "What happened to our son?" Without waiting for her reply, he said: "From now on, you are not alone. I'll be there for everything."

Without opening her eyes, Suja smiled mockingly and said firmly, "I don't need any sympathy for being lonely. I am not one to beg for kindness. I didn't call you for that. It is the last wish of my son to spend a single day with his dad.

Fortunately, it is an organisational commitment for you."

"Suja, why are you speaking like this?" James stared at her. Even then, she had her eyes tightly shut. "Suja, please open your eyes – look at me!" he cried.

Her reply was terse. "No, no. There is an old picture of yours in my mind. I don't want to remove that."

She tried to say something more, but by then Ahmadunni had joined them, and his words silenced her.

"Dear James, allow him to take a breath. Please give the child some space."

It was then that James became aware of his son whom he held clasped close to his chest. He raised the kid's face by his jaw and asked,

"Son, have you heard what your mother said? Haven't you seen that she hasn't even looked at me after this long? Don't you see her with her eyes closed tightly?"

The child didn't answer him. He buried his face in James's chest.

Ahmadunni smiled. "You people got together in twenty-two hours, right? Now you have twenty-four..."

Even then, Suja refused to open her eyes. With a fierce

determination, she said, "No, dear Bappa. I don't have the habit of taking back what I have abandoned."

Ignoring her words, Ahamadunni laughed again.

"Your son may not agree with that habit of yours. Now, you are not alone, you are your son too – it is his need also."

Then he spoke more seriously: "This life is so transient. Don't fight before this lovely child, be his mum and dad."

But Suja remained firm. "No Bappa, I won't return to a place where my love and sacrifice are not recognised."

On hearing that, James said apologetically.

"It was not deliberate, Suja. On that day, somehow those words slipped out of me."

Her tone became very harsh.

"No, no. Whatever you say, whatever you come up with, I won't change my mind."

Ahmadunni was exasperated. He said, "At least for this child? Life is so brief..."

But before Ahmadunni could finish, Sahali began showing signs of distress. He was sweating profusely and his limbs began to tire – he was about to fall when Ahmadunni wailed:

"It seems Allah hasn't heard our prayers. Let's go fast to the hospital..."

Even in his condition, Sahali spoke between gasps: "No, I don't want to go to the hospital. I just want to stay here with my dad."

Hearing this, James felt a kind of satisfaction he had never experienced. It reminded him of Father Gomez and the holy words he used to say: "You love so that you also will be loved."

On the way to the hospital, James looked into Suja's shut eyes as he clasped his son close to his chest. All the way, he whispered to himself: "I love, hence I also will be loved."

James wondered if his soliloquy was a bit louder than

needed, for he saw a question hiding in the lips of his near-unconscious son.

"Dad, what would be your last wish – as someone who grants the last wishes of the dying?"

The founder of Magic Lamp, the voluntary organisation which fulfils the last wishes of the dying, muttered his last wish.

"Not just for a single day, not for a single birth, I want to live with you and your mum in all my births."

Suja might have heard that. She may have opened her eyes. James was very sure – where else could this pleasant light spreading from?

the weeping needle

Tears streaming down? Can a needle cry?

Can a mere metal injection syringe acquire eyes, a face, and a human form?

Mathews Varghese, also known as Mathen, was surprised and felt a mix of anxiety and fear at the same time.

Since he had been bedridden after a jeep accident that left his body completely paralysed, he sometimes experienced hallucinations. But Mathan realised with a shock that nothing like this had ever happened before.

A mere needle tip acquires the human form and cries... tears roll down... a hideous, obscure human form emerging from behind...

Mathan tried to console himself: it was just a delusion.

It had been twenty-three months earlier, while walking home from the hospital, that he first experienced such things. While being carried on a stretcher into an ambulance, two angels were singing hymns! He heard them singing throughout the shaky journey along the potholed road. His heavenly magical journey unfolded on the hands of those angels – until it ended with Mary's wrathful outburst:

"What should the doctors do if they find out that the spinal cord has been cut and the patient has lost mobility? Should they send him home, asking the family to turn him over and apply cream and talcum powder intermittently? Is that okay?"

Mary was the wife of his son, Yohannan. She used to speak

very softly, like an angel, but her words had since become terribly harsh.

What was it – anger, scolding or curses?

Yohannan tried to placate her as she spread the grass mat on the wooden cot and laid Mathan on it.

"What can I do? He's my father, can I just throw him away? It doesn't seem like he will take long to..."

Mary didn't mince her words when Mathan paused halfway. "I can't do this. The son has to look after his dad..."

Mathan didn't hear his answer. Yoshannan knew that Mathan couldn't get up and protest because he was immobile. He could also count it a blessing that his father's vocal cords were paralysed. No matter how badly they treated him, Mathan wouldn't speak a word. It was improbable that he would complain to those who visited – and he didn't.

However badly Mathan was ignored, he did not complain. Most days, his son and daughter-in-law didn't even enter his room. Avarachan, assigned to help him, would come in the morning and sprinkle powder on his back. He poured rice porridge into Mathan's mouth and made him swallow it. The same ceremony was repeated at dusk. Occasionally, Mathan's body was wiped clean. The grass mat was washed only when urine or faeces soiled it.

At those times, Mathan could hear his son or daughter-in-law grumbling outside: "What a stink this is. Will any human being feel like coming in here?" Then the angels' song would descend in his mind, like soothing hymns.

If you have the fragrance of compassion in your heart, you can breathe sweetness even in the stench...

Mathan remembered that his father used to say this too.

When their family migrated from Painadath in Pala to Kallumala in Idukki, his mother was full of complaints. For every word of hers, his dad would sing the angel's song.

Suffering keeps you alive everywhere, every day and all the time...

Mathan's father took his wife and family to the hillside when cereals were replaced by rubber and tilling by tapping; he was not comfortable with the change. He built a shack in Kallumala and brought everything he saw around him under his control with great resolve. He sweated on till he died. The result was worth it – a nice house and a big farm.

While his four elder brothers turned to agriculture, Mathan showed no interest. That was because of Dr Gomes, the idol of Kallumala. When Mathan saw him, he wanted to become a white-coated health worker. As he could not study medicine, he became a doctor's assistant. When he started the dispensary, he became its all-in-all.

The doctor would go to his native place for three months every year. Then, Mathan's work extended to examination, diagnosis and dispensing medicines. The Tamilians who climbed the mountain to see him, would leave praising the divine grace in the treatment of the 'doctor'.

It was in Dr Gomes' last days that it was discovered he was a fraud. After one of his regular visits to his native place, he returned exhausted. That night he called Mathan close and said: "I want to make a confession."

Mathan, shocked by the strange request, hesitated before suggesting, "Let's go to church in the morning."

"It doesn't need a church or a priest – you are enough. It is not a suggestion or a wish, but an inviolable commandment." Dr Gomes huddled as if in a confessional box and opened his mind to Mathen's ear: "I have cancer. I go home regularly for treatment. Now, there is no escape – it is in its secondary stage, and the cancer has spread to my brain and lungs. My days are numbered. I am a fake doctor who treated people without any medical education. The only thing I had to do with medicine was the time I assisted Dr Terence Bern, a white man, in Munnar..."

Taking a break, Dr Gomes sobbed and continued: "I don't

want to die inch by inch, afflicted with madness or breathing difficulties – the end must come quickly. No-one is waiting for me anywhere. I left my home so long ago that I don't even remember where my native place is. My role as a doctor was assumed after many fraudulent acts. In the meantime, I did many good things and bad things under the cover of this hospital. We don't need this anymore. Don't follow my path."

As Mathan listened with trepidation, Dr Gomes said with extraordinary resolve: "All you need is an overdose injection of insulin to die calmly and painlessly. No need to look for a vein, just inject it into me. I've already given myself enough insulin. If I don't die in an hour or two, inject a little more."

Mathen recalled visiting and injecting sick patients in their homes with Dr Gomes. Sometimes, the doctor even made Mathan administer the injections. But that was for others. Now...

Gomes supplied Mathan with courage: "Don't be afraid. It will seem like a normal death caused by hypoglycaemia."

As Mathan watched on, Gomes grew very tired. He shivered and fainted into death while the hymn of the angels echoed.

Death is sleep.

Sleep to wake up soon... Sleep for awakening...

Mathan had doubts about whether that too was a delusion.

Dr Gomes did not wake up again, but soon, the valley echoed with another refrain: So what if the senior doctor is gone? His disciple, Dr Mathan, is better than the guru.

He had closed the hospital and was about to look for another job, when Mathan heard the local news through many tongues, and the flow of patients resumed.

At that time neither government nor private dispensaries had come to Kallumala or nearby areas. Doctor Mathan became the sole recourse for everyone.

Dr Gomes, from his experience as a doctor's assistant, would often tell Mathan: "Ninety percent of diseases heal on their own with time. Five percent remain unresponsive to treatments. Only the remaining five percent can be cured by medical intervention – and we don't always have the ability to do that. The best treatment is to give comfort and kind words."

That advice was Mathan's strength. First of all, he named the hospital the Dr Gomes Memorial Health Centre. It became a refuge not only for the people of Kallumala, but also for the people of Kambam, Theni, Kallachi and Chittumala, who came uphill from the east. Soon, the illiterate residents of the area began to believe that any disease would be cured by just one touch from Mathan.

There used to be a long line of patients in front of Mathan until the first government dispensary and mission hospital came to Kallumala. Mathan earned a lot –he had a good house and farms. He was financially and socially better off than his farmer brothers. In between, he married Annamma, the daughter of a settler named Kuncheria from Nadukani, and their son Yohannan was born. When Annamma died of malaria, Mathan could only watch helplessly. Yohannan was ten years old at the time. Despite pressure from many, Mathan refused to marry again.

There were many reasons for this. First of all, he could not imagine another woman in Annamma's place. The second thought was that he didn't want Yohannan to be raised by a step-mother. And finally, the special smell emanating from the currency notes brought from the hospital reminded him of the smell between Annamma's breasts – it was intoxicating. That smell did not allow Mathan to think of another woman. Whenever someone insisted he remarry, he would hear the angels' song: *Your spouse has never left you. She is always with you, still...*

Was it a hallucination? By the time he pondered it, his money box had overflowed, and Annamma's lovely scent grew stronger.

It was during that time that Mathan started to visit patients in their homes so as to fill the money box.

It was very profitable. He treated the near-death patients with kind words and vitamin tablets – sometimes, he injected them with water. Some got relief, some lived a little longer, while others succumbed to natural causes.

Mathan's treatment was deemed a resounding success, and the good doctor was given convenience of transportation and double fees. Annamma's scent intoxicated him much more. Then came a task that changed his life forever – a mission for Chinnaswamy.

It had been six months since Theni native Chinnaswamy's father, Kanthaswami, had become bedridden after his spine was broken. Treatments like massaging, *Uzhichil* and *Pizhichil,* and local medicines didn't work. Chinnaswamy pleaded, "The doctor should just visit him and take a look." And so Mathan went there and saw him.

Kanthaswami, who had spent a lifetime working the fields with animals, had been betrayed by his beloved pair of 'Vetti' bulls. One afternoon, while ploughing under the hot sun, the pair broke the yoke from the plough and ran together towards the distant trough. Kanthaswami ran after them, holding the twined ropes around the necks of the bulls in his hands. The last thing Kanthaswami remembered was the ropes snapping when the bulls entered the paddy field, and he fell backward. When he regained consciousness, he smelled peacock oil outside the house. He had fallen with his back on a rock, breaking his spine.

Mathan could not bear the stench when he saw Kanthaswami. The man seemed to have nothing but his eyes – bright, accusing eyes. His back had cracked open and developed sores, probably from being bedridden for such a long time.

Mathan stood there not knowing what to do, when his son

Chinnaswamy made a desperate request: "Don't make my father suffer like this. I have heard from old-timers that Dr Gomes used to give an injection treatment to people like him. Didn't his disciple also learn that technique? Won't you show mercy? Please help us."

Chinnaswamy's demand was unexpected. While Mathan debated whether to resort to Dr Gomes's methods, Chinnaswamy elaborated on the necessity of it:

"There is no-one here to look after my father. My mum is not healthy enough to care for him. Moreover, my marriage, fixed long ago, is being delayed due to his condition. If this is over, everything would be fine. I will give you any amount of money for obliging me..."

During this explanation, Mathan heard the sound of the money box being opened and the scent of Annamma intensity a hundred-fold. He also heard the singing of angels: *Which smell are you looking for among hundreds of smells? Follow only what is right for you.*

You will smell what is destined for you...

Surprising himself, Mathan replied: "I haven't any medicine with me now. Tomorrow I'll return with the medicine."

Hearing that, Chinnaswamy's face lit up with happiness. At the same time, the bulls that had caused Kanthaswami's fall neighed loudly outside.

The next day, when Mathan went to treat Kanthaswami, the butchers were standing outside with ropes. However important the pedigree of the bulls had been, once unfit for ploughing, they were destined for the slaughterhouse. Chinnaswamy, who had been arguing with them, hastily sold the bulls, collected the cash and came inside.

Although Mathan was prepared to administer the injection, Kanthaswanmi writhed in pain and his hands trembled violently.

It was as if Kanthaswami was about to accept something he

didn't want. He showed great resentment and protest despite his failing health and tiredness.

In such cases, Dr Gomes would often say to Mathan, who would stand paralysed with indecision: "Do not listen to the bans of those who cannot return – send them away quickly. One thing is especially important, do not look at the face of the person who receives the needle prick."

After that advice, Mathan used to close his eyes and inject.

Following that teaching, Mathan closed his eyes and saw a formless figure, from which something was overflowing...

Mathan wondered for a moment whether it was tears? Maybe he was hallucinating.

He tried to control his mind.

It took immense effort to steady himself.

He instructed Chinnaswamy, "Don't give him food or water," and the injection process began.

When three syringes were empty, Kanthaswami said something. His son strained to listen to his words, and then explained: "My father said that he wanted to wait until my marriage... he wants to see the face of the bride who comes into the family... After that, my baby."

Mathan felt a terrible tremor within. Unknowingly, he looked at the hollow-eyed face of the old figure. Two stars blazed forth from deep pits...

Mathan was really frightened. He scolded Chinnaswamy for his untimely explanation. "Don't you know that relatives shouldn't stay nearby while I'm treating the patient?"

Over six hundred units of insulin had been pumped into Kanthaswami's body. Within half an hour, every vein in his body would thirst for energy – an unquenchable thirst.

Mathan could not remember anything else. As he hurried out, Chinnaswamy gave him the entire sum he had collection from the butchers.

"I have not counted the money," said Chinnaswamy.

"You should have two thousand three hundred rupees." As he pocketed the money, Mathan fidgeted uneasily.

"When can we expect—" Chinnaswamy stopped halfway.

Mathan replied automatically, "In the morning." Then he added, "Inform the relatives right now that the illness has become more serious."

Mathan returned home with two burning eyes etched into his mind. It was the kind of flame that caused excruciating pain. Even the half bottle of brandy he consumed in one go while on the road, couldn't diminish the heat within.

Mathan felt an overwhelming sense of guilt and self-loathing for breaking Dr Gomes's commandment never to look into the eyes of the dying. The fervour of Kanthaswami's gaze – the pitiable plea in those hollow eyes – would haunt him for the rest of his life. It would follow him like a relentless hound, terrifying him at every turn.

He resolved never to undertake such tasks again. But that resolve was tested when Velunaikkar, a farmer from Kambam, approached him. Mathan owed some debts to Velunaikkar. The farmer said as soon as he came in:

"My ninety-year-old mother has become a huge burden. She doesn't eat, doesn't sleep, and keeps murmuring all the time. She relieves herself wherever she lies. We are four siblings, and we tried taking turns caring for her each week. But as soon as I carry her to one of my siblings' houses, they return her the next day. I tried convincing them about the shared responsibility. It didn't work. I scolded them – even that failed. My wife and children are fed up. Finally, we've decided to consult the doctor."

Mathan tried his best to decline the request, but Velunaikkar was adamant.

"We have taken all precautions. Everyone has been informed that mother is critical. Now if the doctor comes and takes a look, I can put an end to the problem with dignity. I'll pay whatever you demand."

Was it his obligation to Velunaikkar, or the allure of

money that led him to undertake the mission again? Mathan couldn't recall.

When he was prepared to lead the old woman with fourteen grandkids and twenty-nine great grandchildren to the tiredness of injection, he closed his eyes as usual. Then also, Mathan saw a formless figure from the eyes of which something fell down. Mathan completed the task, though he doubted whether it was tears.

It was quite dark when Mathan returned. On the way, he pointed to a heavy hammock slung on a stick, carried on a person's shoulders. Velunaikkar, who came to see him off, said in a low voice: "That is one of my uncles. His elder son is taking him to his younger sister's house. The cloth hammock will be left outside her house, and it will return before dawn to its original place."

Velunaikkar gave him a packet while parting. When he came home and counted the notes: two thousand three hundred rupees. The sum was identical to the first. Mathan couldn't dismiss it as mere coincidence.

He was shocked when Chackochan came from Adimala for the third mission. Now, the father had become a liability to Chackochan and his brothers, who sang the psalm: "The son is a treasure to the father. He is always a saviour."

By the time Chackochan's father, Kunjettan, also known as Kunju Vareethu, made his children rich by working tirelessly in the fields, cultivating crops like pepper and rubber, he was bedridden with paralysis. Kunjettan had five children – four daughters and one son. All the daughters had been married off and now lived in the United States.

Chackochan inherited the family property and his dad, but his main issue lay with his eldest sister.

She was a nurse in America and was due to give birth to a child the next month. Chakochan's mother, Sara Chedatti, a skilled midwife with extensive experience, was the natural choice to assist her daughter. However, with his father confined to bed, there was no way to send his mother overseas. Chackochan's wife was already overwhelmed managing the household and caring for their children. This left only one solution: the removal of Kunjettan. Since he had been ill and confined to his bed for years, a single injection administered discreetly would solve the problem without raising suspicions.

After explaining the matter, Chackochan held out a package. "I have brought your fee. Two thousand three hundred."

More than Chackochan's request and the reasoning, what shocked Mathen was the amount he brought. Who had fixed Mathan's fee for this mission?

Chackochan supplied the answer: "I won't offer less than the amount the Tamilians paid."

Chackochan pushed a wad of notes in Mathan's hand without waiting for an answer or confirmation of his willingness, then walked away. The psalms echoed in Mathan's ears: *A wise son means wealth to his father...*

When that reached a crescendo, an intoxicating smell rose from the packet in his hand. Annamma's enchanting scent.

He'd smelt the same smell when Kunjettan was injected with insulin, and along with it was the presence of the shapeless figure. Mathan also felt the dampness of tears from its absent eyes.

The return journey was on the chariot of that enchanting smell. But the smell disappeared at the sight of the one-eyed Moideenkannu Rawther, who was waiting in the front yard of Mathan's home. He was the intermediary, an agent for anything. It was Rawther who led and somewhat controlled Dr Gomes. It had been a long time since Mathan had seen him. Now he had come with an urgent mission:

Two years previously, Meera Sahib's wife in Meempotti had gone crazy. It was her money that had made Sahib a top businessman – that was the reason for his special place in the community. If the delirious wife got out of his way, he would be at peace and could marry another woman without much fuss. If she died under Mathan's care, no-one would doubt him. Sahib was ready to give Mathan anything for the service.

Mathan was unsure why he accompanied Rawther that day. Was it in the hope of getting more money as reward? Or could he simply not discourage this agent who sought his help for the first time? Why throw him away? Through Rawther could come many more customers – new places, new opportunities. Calculations like these played in his mind.

When he saw the woman chained there, he suddenly thought of Annamma – though because it wasn't his wife's scent that emanated from her, the memory vanished the same instant. Mathan closed his eyes before administering the injection, and in the darkness behind his shut lids, the formless figure appeared, its absent eyes overflowing with tears, and Mathan found himself moist with their dampness.

Once it was done, Rawther did not give Mathan what he was promised. What he received was the fixed amount – two thousand three hundred rupees. Mathan wanted to ask Rawther who fixed the fee at this exact amount? But he did not.

The second agent arrived within two days, probably because Mathan had obeyed Rawther. He was Venkitaraman, otherwise known as Venkiti. The mission was for an Iyer guy, married to a white woman and living in America. His father, Krishna Iyer, an old man, would fall ill whenever he couldn't see his son. Sometimes, he even fainted.

Krishna Iyer's son was born when he was in his fifties, and his wife had died shortly after childbirth. Krishna Iyer had raised his son alone, teaching him everything. But when his son left for a job in America, the father was left behind. Sivamani, a young relative, was tasked with caring for him, but Krishna Iyer's heart yearned only for his son. This longing made him sick. Relatives and friends, including Sivamani, pleaded with the son to stay with his father or take him to The States. But entangled in complicated relationships, the son could not manage it. He visited occasionally but left quickly.

His son got tired as he had to return four or five times a year. He spoke of the problem privately to a village helper close to him. Venkiti's advice was to go on a trip to Poopara, where it was common for accidents to happen. You can reach the top of the hill by going around the valley. On the other side of the hill is a deep gorge.

Unknowingly, an 'unintentional' push could send the father plummeting. An old man dying in an accident would raise no suspicions. Though Venkiti offered to do it himself, the son refused. Doctor Mathan was the next option, for which the son was in complete agreement. But Sivamani, who smelled something, stood in the way.

When Mathan reached Krishna Iyer's village with Venkiti, the house was crowded with people. Krishna Iyer's son had informed the neighbours that a doctor was coming to examine his father's deteriorating health. Venkiti ensured everyone else would be kept out during the inspection. As usual, Mathan felt the presence of the formless figure and the wet touch as he administered the injections. The scent of Annamma wafted in, too.

When the third syringe emptied, Krishna Iyer laughed joyously, clutching his son's hand and said, "The son is the one who saves his father from the hell called Puth." He called "Narayana," and held his son's hands tightly.

When Mathan saw Krishna's hands slackening, he left

the room. The picture of his son Yohannan suddenly came to his mind. Mathan felt overwhelmed for no reason – that had been his first experience during a treatment. Venkiti did not allow him to continue in that vein. He demanded that Mathan should report to the neighbours about Iyer's health condition. Finally, Mathan announced to no-one in particular: "It's serious. I don't think he will last more than a few hours."

"How could he endure that?" the neighbours said. "It is better that he is here with Mathan doctor."

As the villagers' reactions continued that way, Mathan pretended to be busy and hurried away. Venkiti, who went with him, counted the notes and gave him the fee – exactly two thousand and three hundred rupees. He added that he took seven hundred rupees as his commission.

When Venkiti left, a hand pressed tightly on Mathan's shoulder – a fair looking, lanky boy. Mathan looked at him in shock while the boy spoke without a preface: "I am Sivamani, Krishna Iyer's helper. Did you finish off Krishna Iyer?"

Mathan was stunned to hear the unexpected accusation. Before he could recover, Sivamani began to cry.

"Poor Krishna Iyer – he was not ill. His disease was the excess of love for his son..." The boy wept and cursed himself, "Had I been there, I would not have agreed to this. I did not suspect anything when I was sent to town urgently to book a ticket. But when I saw you coming back with Venkiti and listened to your conversation by lurking behind you, I was sure that you are Doctor Mathan and that the story of Krishna Iyer was over..."

Without waiting for an answer, the boy's voice grew firm.

"I could have you arrested by the police for killing my beloved Iyer, but it will be Narayanayan, Iyer's beloved son, who will go to the gallows. That, Iyer won't bear. So I have no voice. No recourse. I want to at least see the corpse before cremation. You'll suffer for this," he said as he stepped back, releasing his grip on Mathan's shoulder. "Maybe, time may depute me for the same. For, I loved him sincerely. He also loved me very much..."

When Sivamani disappeared into the darkness, Mathan felt the darkness spreading within him.

This darkness consumed him for several months, to the point where Mathan couldn't practice his profession.

He only restarted the mission after persistent persuasion from a third agent.

Pazhani approached him with the case of Sundara Manikyam in Kampammett. Manikyam, who had transformed eighteen acres of rocky land into fertile farmland, was old and stubborn, refusing to divide his property among his five children. He made them work like slaves. When his wife died, everyone tried to persuade him to remarry, but he dismissed the idea, claiming that his land and farm were enough for him.

Manikyam, an acute diabetic, despite a festering wound on his leg caused by climbing a rock, continued to walk his land and work tirelessly. Of late, the infection in his wound had become worse, confining him to bed. But still he refused to go to the hospital, fearing that his control could vanish if he did.

The infection was inching up his leg and Manikyam had no idea how long he would have to lie like that. His children wanted Mathan to visit their house and put an end to everything.

When Mathan looked closer, he realised that the gangrene had spread above Manikyam's knees. But his intelligence and memory were as sharp as ever. Ignoring the formless form, the pouring rain and the incessant hymns, Mathan took in the scent of Annamma and started. Then suddenly, as he was injecting the third syringe of insulin, Manikyam said: "I knew that if I didn't come to the hospital, my children would bring home the hospital and the doctor... I have given them that much care..."

Expressing concern that he might not be able speak any further, he paused and continued to address the children standing around him. "I have divided our land equally among you all. The income from the farming has been deposited in separate bank accounts for each of you. The will and passbooks are under my pillow."

His next words shocked everyone: "The doctor's fee has been kept aside. Exactly two thousand three hundred rupees." He stopped a little and blurted out: "There is no commission in this business. My children's money is not to be wasted like that, that's why I myself set apart the exact fee."

He didn't speak after that.

Mathan went home with a lot of embarrassment – he felt as though he had been slapped. He even thought of leaving the job. But as new hospitals came up in Kallumala and medical facilities became widespread, Mathan found himself returning to his old profession to make money, enjoying the intoxicating scent of cash whenever he opened his money box.

Then, one day, Police Inspector Alikunju Mathan, newly transferred to Kallumala, approached him with a completely unexpected request: He had a secret girlfriend in Aluva whose harassment had become unbearable. She was now bedridden with a minor health condition, and the inspector wanted Mathan to 'treat' her.

Mathan hesitated, explaining that his services were only for infirm, elderly patients in nearby areas.

Alikunju's tone turned menacing: "You live in a country where euthanasia is not legal. I have with me every information on the murders committed by you for two thousand and three hundred rupees each.

Expect nothing less than the death penalty."

Mathan began sweating, his heartbeat quickening with fear. He trembled, but soon realised that this was just another police threat.

"You're not a fake doctor, just a health worker. It's not a crime to help diabetics inject insulin or store it. Some of them might have died as their illnesses worsened. None of them complained. Or, at least, it's not your fault."

Alikunju paused and then gestured theatrically. "Of course, I could interpret things differently... but that would depend on your cooperation."

Mathan agreed to cooperate.

Alikunju's secret girlfriend, a pale young woman, was resting in her flat due to excessive bleeding. She looked lovingly at Alikunju as he introduced Mathan as the 'expert doctor'.

When Mathan had finished injecting the third syringe, the girlfriend whispered to Alikunju: "As soon as I recover, I will come to Kallumala..."

The girl didn't come, but a fifteen-year-old boy named Munir arrived instead.

"Take him as a helper. After your death, someone will need to carry on your work, right?" Alikunju was insistent.

When Mathan told him that he didn't need a helper, Alikunju was firm, and he set new terms. "From now on, the doctor's fee will be four thousand rupees. You can take the usual share. Of the one thousand and seven hundred left, one thousand and five hundred is mine, and the rest for Munir. He will talk to the patient's relatives about the fee."

Mathan's medical practice subsequently came under the control of Alikunju. Many of Alikunju's referrals had to be treated irrespective of their age. In rare cases, Mathan had to treat both the witnesses and the plaintiffs. But the true source of his present calamities was the day Alikunju took him to the police quarters to treat a man on the brink of death.

Pointing to the emaciated young man curled up in the

corner of the quarters, Alikunju suggested without any emotion: "The post-mortem should show the death was due to hypoglycaemia."

After assigning Munir to help Mathan, Alikunju left.

However, this time the shapeless figure did not appear. Nor did Mathan hear the psalm of the angels when he started administering the injection. There was no odour from the cash box either. Just as he wondered why, the young man let out a soft moaning sound. He who had been lying still and exhausted until then, suddenly stirred and opened his eyes slightly.

Then, Mathan broke his own rule and looked at the man's face. In that instant, he was scalded by the all-consuming fire in those eyes.

The man asked softly, "Didn't Doctor Mathan understand who I am?"

Mathan did not understand. Searching his memory, he heard a distant echo of a voice.

"We have seen the day you killed Krishna Iyer as the Lord of Death. I introduced myself as Sivamani, and we talked."

Mathan stood shocked, even as the words of Sivamani gained strength.

"Since his son was abroad, the power of attorney of all his properties, including the farms, were in my name. I transferred them as instructed by the inspector and his friends...

Now why should I live?"

That question struck Mathan's chest like a dagger. He had never been in a dilemma like this.

Perhaps sensing his hesitation, Munir pressed him again, "Jab, doctor, jab."

Sivamani's feeble protests were crumpled in Munir's hands. Still, Mathan refused to go back to the mission. For the first time, a force inside him compelled him to refuse.

Seeing his hesitation, Munir raised his voice, mimicking Alikunju's threats. "Countless murders. Capital punishment."

Mathan could no longer control himself.

It was unclear how many syringes were emptied or how much of the medicine entered Sivamani's body. It was Alikunju's orders to Munir that brought Mathan back to the present.

"Pick him up and take him to his residence. Leave the doctor on the way."

The return trip was in Alikunju's private jeep. Munir was the driver. As the jeep descended a curve, Sivamani, lying unconscious in the back, suddenly reached forward and wrapped his hands around Munir's neck.

The jeep careened out of control.

When he regained consciousness, his son Yohannan and daughter-in-law Mary were by his bed. Yohannan prayed softly, thanking God that the jeep, which had rolled down the curve, had turned to dust.

Mathan might have survived due to sheer luck, but his speech was gone. He couldn't move his limbs eithers.

A week later, after various tests, the doctor revealed the shocking fact: "The spinal cord is severed. Your future mobility is doubtful..." The following words were just to console him. "Let's wait. Miracles are not rare in medical science."

Mathan spent a month in the hospital, learning about his companions in the accident. Munir had died, the jeep's steering wheel having pierced his chest. Sivamani, though gravely injured, survived. After initial treatment, his relatives had taken him to a hospital in Madurai.

How had Sivamani survived?

"I escaped," came the reply.

The needlepoint was talking.

It was no delusion, the words were clear.

"For this single day – for such a meeting – I was spared..."
Sivamani's vague form was behind the needle!

This was not an illusion. That form was obvious now, and it spoke.

"I was put on a glucose drip because of the accident and ensuing hospitalisation. The hypoglycaemia caused by the overdose of insulin did not kill me, so there was no need for a post-mortem."

The memory of the scene at the police quarters flashed through Mathan's mind, but his curiosity about Sivamani's survival and presence overpowered it.

Sivamani, as if reading Mathan's thoughts, continued. "Your son Yohannan brought me here."

After a moment of silence, Sivamani continued: "Within the last two years, others have replaced the vacuum created by Doctor Mathan – here and elsewhere. When people from here go for treatment to the Kampam and Theni area, they come here for the same. So your son, who sought the doctor there, ended up in the hands of our Venkiti. Venkiti knew I wanted to see you. Perhaps it was someone's command that brought you here with Yohannan through him... and it was my fate to obey."

Sivamani looked up, closed his eyes for a moment, then raised his right hand: "I have lots of syringes and insulin. I don't need anyone else's help to jab you, who are already immobile."

Mathan was gripped by fear. Even though he could not call out – "My son!" He felt desperate at having no voice.

Somewhere, that unspoken cry was heard. Its response came swiftly: *Whatever is given, he returns tenfold – whether love, mercy, or care. No-one leaves without reaping what they've sown. Without harvest, there is no salvation.*

Mathan felt that the day of judgment had come near.

The faces of all his victims, from Doctor Gomes to Sivamani, flashed before his mind. Mathan also saw the innumerable needle points that had pierced them. Now all of them gathered around the bed with the syringes and prepared for the injection. Amid the chaos, Sivamani raised his voice, "Don't think death will come easily, Doctor Mathan. You are mistaken. Believing you've been injected, your son will place you in a coffin, carry you in a hearse to the cemetery, and bury you alive in untouched soil. Or, if signs of life are noticed during the last sacrament at the gravesite, you'll be brought back here, only to lie waiting for eternity..."

Mathan's heart melted. Was it a prayer that stuck in his throat? Then something else cut through his fears – a booming revelation: *Everything sprouts from the soil. Only what sprouts grows.*

Mathan now clearly saw the origin of that booming noise. The shapeless figure that witnessed his every treatment now revealed itself – the shape of the shapeless figure! Mathan recognised it, rising from the soil and reaching toward the sky.

At that realisation, as a helpless Mathan watched, Sivamani lifted the syringe with one hand and slowly pressed it...

Mathan was convinced when he saw droplets of medicine falling in a certain rhythm.

It was not the medicine that fell at all, but tears. The needle was crying.

A mere metal hypodermic needle had acquired eyes, a face, and a human form.

sinking flagpole

An abundance of rice and fish. Vegetables like spinach, bottle gourd, bitter gourd and *brinjal*. To cover sundry expenses, there are coconuts to be sold. Ample rains and plenty of water. Not only that, but there are also three rivers which, twice a year during *Thulam* and *Edavam*, cleanse the land during the monsoon rains.

Should Parameswaran, a native of Kuttanad, trade all this for a box-like apartment in Texas, where the sky and earth are invisible?

After his mother's passing, Parameswaran invited his father to live with him – but his father was looking for excuses to decline.

On the harvest day, after a couple of glasses of toddy and some *karimeen* fish, his dad opened up.

"Will we get *punnellu* and *pallathi* fish curry in Texas? Will I be able to see tender toddy and *karimeen*? Are there unending paddy fields and gentle breezes that caress us? The limitless sky and the lake touching the horizon? Is there a breeze that cools us even after walking miles in between the fields? Will there be the smell of new rice and the softness of mud? Are there Mayilan and Mayili, the children of this soil? My neighbours? This soil in which your mum is buried?"

Then he placed his right hand on his chest and declared, "I am a Kuttanadan. I'm the mud and earth of Kuttanad. The smell of this mud is the breath of my life. Once it stops, I won't be here."

He smiled broadly and leaned back on his easy chair. After a few moments, the faint hum of his snoring was heard. Their caretaker, Kurup, had advised Parameswaran even as he cleaned the compound: "No need to pressurise him. As far as I can understand, if he leaves this place and goes to the US, it would be like a prison sentence."

However, twenty years later, the same Kesava Kaimal, who was once adamant about staying in Kuttanad, and his aide Kurup, who supported him then, now claimed that everything has changed.

"Kuttanad has undergone a sea change. He is all set to come with you... He has already told everyone that he will go to the US."

The revelation was unexpected and shocking for Parameswaran. He had been planning to bring his twelve- and fourteen-year-old daughters to live with his father in Kuttanad, as his wife and her relatives advised him that girls beyond that age might go astray and lose their culture and traditions if they stayed on in the US. He had already made arrangements for that – securing admission for his children in a convent school in Alappuzha.

Parameswaran had kept his plans a secret, intending to surprise his dad. His father had always been proud of their self-sufficiency, saying, "We can live happily with just the money from selling our hay. Why should I be a servant to the white man?"

But now, his dad dropped a bombshell, leaving Parameswaran stunned.

Even during his last visit home, he had never divulged such a wish. Parameswaran thought of asking him directly the reason for the sudden change of mind but was afraid his father might think he was unwilling to take him to the US. Instead, he asked Kurup, who replied with a single word.

"Gone."

As he couldn't understand the meaning of the word, Parameswaran asked again, and Kurup opened up.

"Your father loved Kuttanad. But that Kuttanad is fading fast from the universe itself... He didn't have it in him to see the end."

Kurup was unwilling to speak any further. Parameswaran didn't share his concerns with his wife, thinking he would inform her later.

The next morning, his father asked him if he had any special plans for the day. When Parameswaran replied that he didn't, his father said: "Let's go somewhere."

"Where to, Dad?"

"Nowhere in particular. Let's go west till the Pookaitha canal, east up to Veliyanadu, in the south to Veeyaapuram, and up to Thanneermukkam in the north. If possible, let's go visit Kumarakam and Thottapally too..."

Parameswaran was very happy with the suggestion to explore Kuttanad, both upper and lower. "Shall we take my wife and children along? It's a full day outing, after all."

Without any change in expression, his dad said: "No, no. It's not a full day programme – three hours at the most..." Finally, he relented, "All right, let's take them along."

A week was hardly enough time to explore Kuttanad thoroughly, but Parameswaran's dad claimed they could do it in just three hours! Parameswaran was surprised but suspected his father had a plan in mind, so he kept quiet.

Though he visited Kuttanad every year, Parameswaran hadn't seen the place thoroughly since he was fifteen. Whenever he returned home, he spent the first day with his dad. The following days would be a whirlwind of visits to relatives and old classmates in Alappuzha, Ernakulam, Haippad, Changanassery, and Thiruvalla. He would try to avoid upsetting anyone during his short vacation. On the day of his departure, he'd stay home all day.

Amidst this hectic schedule, when would he find time to explore his native place? In between, might he have time to roam?

Parameshwaran felt a secret pleasure that his dad himself took the pains to arrange for the trip. He might even get a chance to discuss his children's plans with his dad during the journey.

Travelling by car, his wife, Vanaja, and his children were very excited to see the native place. Though broken at places, the road was tarred and broad. When Parameshwaran was a student, it would take an entire day to reach his aunt's home in Veeyapuram as they had to cross fourteen paddy fields and take two ferries. Now, the fields were hardly visible, replaced by remnants of paddy fields, canals covered with hyacinth flowers, swamps, and piles of earth. The bridges had made the ferries almost invisible.

As they drove, Parameswaran spotted three white cranes on the parapet of a long bridge, reminding him of his uncle. Uncle Kuttan was an expert in snaring cranes. He would roam the fields of Cheruthana, Aanari, and Payipad with a locally made gun and a bag filled with gravel, returning with four or five cranes.

During one school vacation, Parameshwaran asked his uncle if he could teach him how to catch a crane.

"Why not? You need to take a little butter with you. Put butter on the head of the crane which is sunbathing on the ridge of the paddy field, its stomach full of fish. In the hot sun, the butter will melt and fall into its eyes, blinding it. Then you can go behind and catch it."

Believing him, Parameswaran went to the field with butter one day. His uncle followed him, laughing.

"You're so stupid!" his uncle said. "Will the crane sit there for you to put the butter on its head? Come on, I'll show you."

Uncle Kuttan aimed his gun at the group of cranes pecking

at the orange chromide fish writhing in the water on the dried-up field. The gravel bullets flew, and three cranes fell.

"Only three cranes – you won't see a group with four of them," Uncle Kuttan had said.

Now, as they journeyed on, Parameswaran, who had been silent until then, spoke up, "Where have all the cranes gone?"

Parameswaran's eyes sparkled with curiosity, and his father, sensing his eagerness, replied, "If cranes want to come, they need fish to eat, and if they want fish, they need water. Did you see any fields with water on this trip?"

Parameswaran shook his head. "No, all we saw were canals choked with hyacinth, backwaters strewn with oil from houseboats, and weedy fields. Most of the fields have been restored, and the few remaining empty ones are being filled up too. Even concrete structures are being built on them."

Not only the little orange chromide fish, but also tasty varieties of catfish – Kari, Kouri, Mushi, and Karati – might be lying buried under that soil, their silent screams echoing through the desolate landscape. The white cranes that once feasted on them now lurked in hiding, never to emerge again.

As the car turned a bend and continued down another road, Parameswaran's father announced, "We've covered Veeyapuram – now we're heading back. We'll take the main road via Veliyanad to Kumarakom, then proceed to Thanneermukkam, visit Thottapalli, and return home via Ambalapuzha."

The car rolled on, but Parameswaran's thoughts drifted elsewhere. Where were the *Punja* fields where *Mundaka* paddy seeds first sprouted? And the reclaimed lands where *Kolappala* – a rice variety thriving in water up to two and a half metres deep –flourished? He missed the sight of paddy nurseries and the sowers at work.

Nooru para padam, where a hundred *para*[3] of paddy seeds could be sown, had been somewhere here. The house

---

3. A traditional unit of measurement for paddy

of Parambil Papi, the farmer who was found dead, poisoned by *furadan* after all his paddy crops were destroyed by *aphids*, also once stood here. Nothing was recognisable.

Where were the workers who had drained the water in the field by pedalling the wooden water wheel? Parameswaran remembered climbing onto one with twenty-four paddles, manned by six, and another with twelve paddles and two workers. In their stead, there were now water pumps and engine sheds; and the fields, once crisscrossed with ducts smelling of grease and kerosene, were no more.

The *puttu* shops that had dotted the bunds had disappeared. What a treat it had been to eat steaming hot *puttu* with pea curry early in the morning, in the middle of the fields!

Where were the paddy threshing grounds where he stayed with his father during the harvest season when he was a teenager? Where were the tree houses in which they had taken refuge when the waters rose? Had the paddy fields, where one could walk and inhale the sweet scent of the crop, also vanished? Or have they simply driven past them all?

Nothing seemed familiar anymore.

"Hi, that's a houseboat!"

Parameswaran's elder daughter, Arunima pointed to a creek, and his father told him to stop the car.

Stopping the car on the bank of the canal, Parameswaran saw the sign board of a resort. He remembered that there used to be a duck farm here. Thankachhan or Paulos would come from afar with their flocks of ducks. They would encircle the birds with nets to keep them safe. The harvested fields needed no rent for duck-grazing; but in one-*para* paddy fields, ten eggs had been the amount to be paid to the families for keeping the ducks for one day. Watching the ducks swim, pecking at rice grains and tiny fish, had been a joy – they were like living, moving blossoms across the landscape. Now, though, no ducks were in sight. Where would one find both paddy and fish anymore?

"The whole of Kuttanad, which used to grow paddy, is full of such resorts and houseboats. Is it possible for fish to survive or spawn in oil-soaked water?" spoke Kaimal, in a tone of complaint.

On hearing this, an old policeman emerged from the resort and asked, "Isn't that Kaimal sir? What brings you here?"

Kaimal replied that he was out for a trip with his son and grandchildren and asked Parameswaran to start the car. The policeman, who was intoxicated, did not allow them to move.

Parameswaran found it unbelievable when the man explained, "Don't you know? Something happened yesterday, just like last week."

The policeman went on to describe how a gang had abducted three schoolgirls, forcing them onto a houseboat where they were assaulted. The girls knew only that they had been violated on a houseboat, without knowing which one. The policeman added with a sneer, "You know, there are policemen to investigate..."

Vanaja, clutching her daughters tightly, whispered in fear, "It gives me the jitters."

Ignoring her unease, the policeman was about to elaborate on the previous week's incident when Kaimal urged them to leave.

Parameswaran pulled away, and with the children oblivious to the conversation, Kaimal recounted what happened the previous week.

"They were serial actresses. Teenagers, too... They say it was almost like a movie shoot. They had no complaints as such, but when surrounded by the natives, they screamed it was rape..."

As the car drove along, its tires crunched over discarded plastic bottles littering the road. Parameswaran noticed that plastic bottles had replaced the traditional paddy stacks in many areas. Empty plastic packets resembled straw bales, a poignant reminder of the changing landscape.

Kaimal let out a deep sigh as they drove.

"Upper Kuttanad has almost vanished, and Lower Kuttanad is not far behind."

When they reached Kumarakam, Parameswaran was amazed to see resorts, hotels, houseboats – everywhere.

During his school days, Parameswaran used to visit Kumarakam with his mother at least twice a year to meet Kumarakam Kunjamma, also known as Saraswathy Kunjamma. His mother was very attached to her youngest sister, who returned her love with the same intensity. Her culinary specialty was *ooppa* (a small fish) and pickerel cooked dry with tamarind leaves and thick *kalan* (a sour curry) served with *punja* rice.

While serving them, Kunjamma would fondly repeat: "When the waterbird screamed, I thought my sister would come."

Kaimal murmured something. When asked what he said, he repeated: "None of the waterbirds are the same as they used to be. Just look – are there any fishermen, or those who catch fish with fishing nets?"

That's when Parameswaran noticed. There were no fishermen waiting at the shore with big carps and bluespot mullet as in the past. No fishermen walked about with casting nets. There were no people going out with bamboo snares to catch *ooppa*.

"The lake is filled with garbage... Fish that used to be plentiful are scarce today. If they catch anything, they will be bought in full by the resort people for foreigners. Even the small fish that the locals rarely get have lost their old taste."

There was disappointment in Kaimal's voice.

When they crossed the water-hyacinth-covered canals and reached the smelly water, Kaimal said: "This is the old Methran (Metropolitan) Kayal where we had the best crops.

The visionary bishop foresaw the food shortages and leased this lake from the Maharaja for rice cultivation. He looked for hardworking men in his diocese, drained the lake and sowed paddy with them. The yield was one hundred *meni* – a measure equal to one hundred times what was sown."

There has been no cultivation for the past three years in this 417-acre lake, because, they say, the backwaters were bought from the farmers at a high price by non-farmers. Their goal is lake restoration to make a tourist centre. The belly of this lake, once pregnant with paddy grains, is being split open and filled with sand from hilltops to make eighteen golf courses, along with hotels, bars, shopping malls and villas. Thus, this will become a modern city."

Seeing his father struggling for words, Parmeswaran asked, "There is a law in Kerala saying paddy fields should not be converted or sold for purposes other than rice cultivation. How will this happen?"

Kaimal cried helplessly, "Aren't we clever enough to create loopholes in any law? The ulterior motive of those who bought the fields and left them fallow is to convince the authorities that their land has become unfit for cultivation, and so they should be allowed to use the land for any other purpose."

"Who bought this?"

"Who knows? Not only this – I hear a 300-acre paddy field in the 10,000-acre MN Block was sold. It is also said that a part of the sixty-acre Thumpe Kayal has been sold. The adjacent Maran Kayal is ready for sale. More than 300 acres in Marthandam lake had been earmarked for reclamation. Rani and Chithira backwaters are left barren without paddy cultivation. The purpose is the same. Meanwhile, I heard that someone bought a good chunk of Rani Kayal. Ponnadan Kayal and Nalupanku Kayal have also been left barren by similar buyers..."

Kaimal's voice was overcome with sobs as he continued: "The coal lands lay barren, still seething with anger at the vengeful destruction of the fruits of a great man's labour. An adventurous farmer named Joseph Murikkan achieved a historic feat by carving out three massive backwater paddy fields – the 900-acre Chithira, the 650-acre Marthandam, and the 600-acre Rani – from the vast expanse of Vembanad Kayal. Murikkan's innovative approach involved raking in the stumps, covering them with coconut leaves, filling them with mud to construct a bund, and then draining the water to prepare the fields for cultivation. The sediment deposited over the years was more than enough as manure.

"The lake acknowledged Murikkan's hard work with great respect. The harvest of rice was hundred times the measure of seeds sown. The rice shortage in Kuttanad disappeared. Since hard work was necessary for paddy cultivation, the labourers got constant work. But Kuttanad was unfortunate in retaining that luck. The first Communist government seized Murikkan's backwaters through the land reform law, distributing it among people who did not know what agriculture meant.

"When it was clear that they could not cultivate them, Rani, Chithira and Marthandam lake were handed over to government officials. Would they be comfortable with the sliminess of the mud and the smell of the soil? They did not know about seed quality, sapling strength and the stages of paddy growth.

"When the lands that had yielded a hundred-*meni* crops for three and a half decades were insulted by neglect, Vembanad lake took them back with vengeance. At least some of the Communist leaders who masterminded that great crime might privately regret it today – confessing they could have at least given the reclaimed fields the same concessions as plantations.

"Can these backwaters, abandoned for decades, have inheritors now? Who has the right to sell them? Even now, they are being sold!"

Kaimal's distress unabated, he added with hope, "Gauri Amma, who sees everything today, would surely feel guilty, at least in private. She is that honest..."

After that, Kaimal did not speak for a long time.

When we reached Thanneermukkam, he burst out, "This is

the curse of Kuttanad. Why should man stop the natural flow of nature? Here was nature's arrangement to wash away all the waste from Kuttanad. After it was stopped by the bund, Kuttanad became a whirlpool of waste. From the fertiliser used in paddy fields to the diesel and kerosene spewed by houseboats to human excrement – everything piles up there. A similar path of nature was there in Thottapalli. That too has been closed."

Kaimal pointed it out without delay.

"During the heavy rains, the estuary will be cut here. Even then, the water flowing in is from the upper regions. The mountain waters, laden with nutrient-rich silt, flow through three rivers to fertilise the land of Kuttanad..."

As they drove back via Ambalapuzha and Thakazhi, Parmeswaran's eldest daughter, who had been silent until then, asked, "Is this the wonderland?"

Kaimal asked Parmeswaran what she meant. Parmeswaran had not seen the Aayirappara and Pathinaalayirappara – fields where 1,000 and 14,000 *para* of paddy were grown, respectively.

If that had also disappeared, it was better not to ask – better not to hurt him. Instead he asked why Kaimal had remained silent so far about the *vallam kali* – the boat race and farmer's festival celebrating the harvest. He complained that Kaimal hadn't shown them the boat race venues, making special mention of Punnamada, Paipad, Champakulam, and Neerettupuram boat races.

"Those are famous water festivals," said Kaimal. "I only know of the farm labourer's little country boat."

His voice had the tone of a rebel.

There used to be a *chundan vallam* (a snake boat) in the manor house, so, Parmeswaran wondered why his dad was being so evasive. But Kaimal changed the subject.

"You didn't say, what wonderland did she mean?"

Parameswaran explained in detail.

"The teacher asked the children in her class in the US to write a note about their homeland. Do you know what she had written, maybe from what she overheard?"

"No, tell me."

"Tell him, dear daughter. Grandpa wants to know."

Parameswaran translated to him her heavily accented American English: "My native place is Kuttanad, in the state of Kerala in India, a country in the continent of Asia. It lies below sea level.

The industrious natives construct bunds, drain the backwaters and engage in cultivation. Fish are grown between paddy fields. There are coconut trees and vegetables on bunds. Great harvests. To celebrate its heady success, water festivals are held, and they provide for a captivating spectacle. Three rivers and many canals wash my native land clean. The greenery of prosperity is everywhere. My self-sufficient homeland is a symbol of man's triumph which was made by his partnership with nature."

The teacher liked this note very much. She titled it 'Wonderland' and asked the girl, "Will you take me to this land of yours?"

Kaimal patted his granddaughter's cheek and said, "Smart girl," then told Parameswaran to stop the car.

They were almost home. Parameswaran wondered what was so urgent when his father opened the car door and walked out.

Kaimal walked over to the tipper lorry parked at an incline towards the Pookkayal lake that stretched up to the house. He returned after talking to the driver for a long time.

Holding the car door, Kaimal sighed involuntarily. "The Pookkayal is also being reclaimed."

He remained silent for a long time, then finally spoke to no-one in particular, "Our old Comrade Sarasan has taken the contract to fill this lake by bringing down the Athiru Mala hill on the eastern border of the Kottayam and Idukki districts. Sarasan, who once led the struggle against the reclamation of backwaters in Kuttanad, is now a contractor. At first he worked as a flag-bearer – a worker who passes signals with a flag for when to go to work, eat at breaks, and stop work. Later, he became a chit issuer, managing access for tractors and harvesters on the fields they once blocked.

"The same person who started the agitation against reclamation is now filling them with sand. The place selected for the beginning of the reclamation is the area around that flagpole. His driver says that the lake was bought by someone in a foreign country, and they are adamant about reclamation! So, Sarasan is camping there to bring down Athirumala with about one hundred tippers at his command..."

Kaimal wanted to say something more. But, then his granddaughter excitedly called out, "Squirrel... Squirrel!"

She liked squirrels. Pictures of squirrels of all species adorn her room, where her extra subject was zoology. She had spotted a squirrel somewhere.

Everyone, including her father, turned to look where she pointed.

Beyond her index finger, a baby squirrel clung to the centre of a flagpole, rising from the water where the soil fell from the tipper!

"*Malayannan!*" she cried in panic. "When it sees water, it gets scared. That is why it is not jumping down to safety!"

That's right, Parameshwaran understood. It was the baby of a giant squirrel. But how did a giant squirrel from the forest or mountain end up in Kuttanad, a water-logged place?

The driver, noticing everyone's gaze, approached the car and asked about the commotion. Upon learning about the mountain squirrel on the flagpole, he chuckled: "It must have come with the soil knocked down from the mountain. One or two like this can be seen in every load."

"It's an endangered species." Parmeshwaran's daughter exclaimed as she got out of the car. She observed the baby squirrel and said fearfully, "Dad, we must do something immediately. Here is another big problem."

She pointed to the tip of the flagpole where a red flag fluttered above her index finger. It was the same red flag tied by Comrade Sarasan when he had started the agitation.

She explained that giant squirrels are equally afraid of the colour red and of water. In the wild, during the season of flame tree blooms, they would only come out when all the flowers had withered – they were that scared of the colour red!

The baby squirrel was stuck in the middle of the flagpole, unable to climb up or down. If you tried to save it, it might loosen its hold, jump down and drown. Parameshwaran decided it best to leave the baby squirrel to its fate and return home.

However, his daughter insisted that they must save it somehow. Her father persuaded her, asking whether they should try to save it only to shorten its lifespan. Eventually, he coaxed her back into the car.

The family remained silent until they reached home.

Stepping onto the porch, Kaimal said, "This is the new Kuttanad. Didn't you ask Kurup yesterday what was the reason for my change of heart? This trip was to convince you of the reasons."

Kaimal leaned back in the armchair. Parameswaran wondered if he had dozed off.

It was during this siesta that Kaimal spoke incoherently like a drunkard, though he was not drunk.

"A ball... a ball that bounced off the golf course at reclaimed Methran Kayal, hit me on the head... Terrible pain..."

Parameswaran shook him and called out, "Dad."

He didn't respond and continued: "A bottle... a liquor bottle taken from a city bar in reclaimed Marthandam Kayal, hit the place where your mother's bones are kept... her skeleton got broken..."

No matter how much Parameswaran called, his father did not come back to his senses.

"That mountain squirrel came to my field with its entire clan... destroyed all the paddy..."

Parameshwaran was very frightened. "What has happened to Dad?"

Taking water from the *kindi*, Parameshwaran splashed it on his father's face.

Suddenly his dad woke up and said hesitantly:

"I dozed off. I had a bad dream..."

That was only a one-minute break from sleep. Yet, saying he was very tired, he dozed off and his lips whispered as before.

"I see... Kuttanad without paddy and fish... Kuttanad without vegetables and coconuts... Kuttanad a whirlpool of garbage... Kuttanad is drowned by the monsoon rains and the mountain water rushing in through the three raging rivers..."

Witnessing the distress of his father, Parameswaran made a firm decision. Suddenly, very unexpectedly, his father's fanciful images came true – Kuttanad drowned in a sewage flood!

Above the rising water level, which submerged everything, only the flagpole stood tall. In the middle of it, the giant squirrel clung, unable to move.

But that was not what shocked Parameswaran. The baby squirrel's sharp young teeth were holding between them a man! Parameswaran looked carefully despite his shock, and realised that it was Comrade Sarasan, washed in by the mountain flood. His lips, which had turned a terrible red, finally became black and dark, repeating his father's words with a slight modification:

"No soil... no mountain... no rice... no fish…"

silent invasion

At the temple premises, under the shade of the banyan tree, where serpent idols were arranged in solemn stillness, sat a man who seemed almost like another idol. Around his neck hung a black cord, heavy like a garland for *puja*. A very curious scene, indeed!

As I circumambulated the temple, I couldn't help but notice it – the cord had a small metal piece engraved with something on it. My curiosity knew no bounds. On my next turn, I stopped in front of him and carefully read the inscription: Rudrabhoomi.

The word hit me like a spark, igniting a memory buried deep in the recesses of my mind. That word was familiar to me – something I had once known but long forgotten.

And then, it all came back to me. Rudrabhoomi was the name of a crematorium that had only existed in the imagination of my dear friend Sheshadri.

I still remember the day he spoke of it: we had just left the mutt after attending a discourse on life after death. Sheshadri had turned to me suddenly, his voice carrying an unshakable resolve.

"I have a dream," he said. "I want to build a crematorium called Rudrabhoomi. It's more than a dream – it's a family duty. My grandfather, Ramanatha Shastri, entrusted the task to my father, but he couldn't see it through. So now it's up to me to fulfil the commitment of generations."

For Sheshadri, this was no passing fancy – it was his mission. I had laughed at his strange ambition back then, but he had smiled and said, "Keep this between us." I promised I would. Nobody else knew about it.

And then, there he sat. The man who once dreamed of Rudrabhoomi, sitting in its imagined shadow, the name itself hanging from his neck. What had brought him to this?

As I stood observing the man from the circumambulatory path, Vasukuttan, the temple worker, approached me hastily.

"Sir, what are you staring at? Do you recognise the man sitting there? That's our Shesha Swami!"

I couldn't believe my ears. Could this truly be Harihara Ananta Sheshadri my old classmate – also son of the renowned Ananta Shastri, a blemish-free communist and a great vedic scholar at the same time, who lived at Kundannoor's First Puthenthara Street? The same Sheshadri, who was once known for his integrity and brilliance, was the person who looked like a madman under the banyan tree? Could someone truly transform himself so completely within just three years?

The last time I saw him, Sheshadri had been the senior manager of the Broadway branch of the State Bank. I had gone there for some business and was genuinely amazed at his efficiency and sharpness. As I was about to leave, Sheshadri had spoken to me privately.

"Next Sunday is Alamelu's wedding. You know, there's no need for formalities between us. If you're free, do come to the mutt. You'll also get to see my father."

I didn't ask why Alamelu's wedding had taken so long to happen. Sheshadri and I had studied together at the same school. His younger sister, Alamelu was a charming and intelligent girl. Then there was Venki – short for Venkateshwaran – a man of few words, and finally, Balu, or Balasubrahmanyam, who was always silent. The five of us formed a close-knit group, always together.

Alamelu's wedding rituals had become a kind of

never-ending story. I joined the function at one of its many phases. I spent many hours there and met Ananta Shastri while I was on my way back. He looked frail and weak. Without any preamble, he said to me:

"Once Alamelu is gone, it will just be Sheshu and I left here. My end is near. You must convince Sheshu to get married."

Having lost his wife at an early age, Shastri had dedicated his life to raising his two children. His concern for Sheshu was only natural. But when it came to marriage, Sheshu was not one to agree with his father. For him, a wife and children represented nothing but responsibilities and burdens.

"I have my job at the bank to keep me occupied," Sheshu had told me. "From nine in the morning to eight at night, my work consumes me completely. Everything else fades into the background. This busy schedule gives me a kind of inexplicable joy."

I still remember the way he had laughed when he said, "Maybe it's the same kind of high you might get from alcohol, fine food, or passionate love. That's what my work gives me now."

It was no use trying to speak to him further. Sheshadri had always been a man of his words – resolute and unwavering. This trait had been evident even during our school days. Time had only strengthened it.

As for me, after completing my schooling, my parents moved to the city. I followed them, pursuing higher studies and eventually working abroad. Visits to my hometown were rare. And whenever I did return, it was mainly to visit the old temple and, of course, to meet Sheshadri. Vasukkutty, who juggled multiple jobs, once mentioned how the temple, not yet taken over by the Devaswom Board, barely managed its daily rituals.

Vasukkuttan continued talking, but I could only half-listen, lost in thoughts of Sheshadri.

"Land prices have skyrocketed here. Everyone is selling

their land and leaving. After the Shastris passed away, the *agraharams* (Brahmin houses) in Puthentheruvu were sold for high prices. The villagers moved to Kalpathy or Mailapoor. Leading all that was Sheshu Swami.

"Two or three years ago, Sheshu left his bank job and took up a significant role related to real estate. Then something happened – no-one knows exactly what. About a month and a half ago, one early morning, he suddenly came running to the temple like a madman. He settled under the banyan tree among the serpent idols and hasn't moved since. He speaks to no-one. Some say it's penance or meditation, while others claim it's madness. Either way, no-one bothers him. And after all, isn't this temple part of the Swami mutt's legacy?"

Although I could hear Vasukkutty's words, my attention was fixed on Sheshadri. He sat there under the banyan tree. I thought he opened his eyes and looked at me sometime in between – or was it my imagination?

No matter what, I couldn't bring myself to leave Sheshadri like that.

Seeing me linger there, Vasukkuttan remarked, "Sir, I've sold everything here and now live in Koothattukulam. If I leave now, I can find a ride back..." When I didn't respond, he asked again, "Can I leave? If I delay, I might miss my ride..."

Without waiting for my reply, Vasukkuttan began walking away. Then, it was just Sheshadri and me under the banyan tree.

"Sheshu..." I called softly.

He didn't seem to hear me.

I moved closer and spoke again, "Sheshu, don't you recognise me?"

Still, he didn't open his eyes.

Finally, I said, "Sheshu, I can't leave you like this. That's why I stayed. There's no-one else here but us. If you're meditating, stay as you are – I won't disturb you. But if you are ill, let me take you to a hospital."

Even then, there was no reaction. Repeating my questions and requests yielded nothing. Finally, exasperated, I said,

"I'm leaving..."

At that, Sheshadri opened his eyes. His face contorted with emotion, and his lips quivered.

"I'm scared," he whispered.

I stepped closer and placed a hand on his shoulder. His body was trembling, shaking like a leaf.

"Sheshu, what are you afraid of? What's going on? Is it some kind of illness? If it is—" He cut me off before I could finish.

"No. I'm not sick. It's just... I'm scared."

"That doesn't sound right, Sheshu. Fear like this – it could be a sign of something. Come on, get up. Let's go see a doctor."

"No! It's not some mental illness," he said, almost panicked. "This fear is for real."

"Alright, then tell me. What is it? What's making you so afraid?"

He looked around cautiously, as if someone might overhear, and then leaned in closer. In a voice barely louder than a whisper, he said,

"I'm afraid of everyone... everything. At the height of fear, it felt like the only safe place left was within the temple walls of goddess Bhuvaneswari. That's why I came here.

They won't follow me here."

His words left me uneasy. It was clear something was seriously wrong with him. Whatever it was, I had to help him, somehow. I decided I needed to take him to a psychiatrist.

"Sheshu, I'm here with you now, you know," I said gently but firmly. "Let's step outside, okay? Whatever's troubling you, we'll get to the bottom of it. The way you look, your attire... Let's get you back to being the Sheshadri I know – the real you."

At that, he looked at me sharply. Then, in a surprisingly calm tone, he said,

"You think I'm mad or on the verge of it, don't you? I tell you, I'm not. I'm perfectly fine. You'll see once I tell you everything."

"Then tell me, Sheshu. Whatever it is, I'm here. I'll listen."

"You don't understand," he said, shaking his head. "If I tell you, you'll hate me. You might even curse me. And maybe... maybe it'll ruin your peace of mind too."

I placed my hand on his shoulders again, reassuringly.

"Sheshu, no matter what it is, I won't turn my back on you. Just tell me."

He hesitated for a moment, then sat behind the serpent idols beneath the banyan tree, as though fearing something. He arranged space and beckoned me to sit beside him.

When I did, he grabbed my hands tightly, like someone clutching onto a lifeline. His words came out haltingly at first, filled with anguish and regret. Slowly, piece by piece, he began to share his story.

Sheshu had been one of the most trusted managers at the State Bank. His transfer from Bombay to the Broadway branch had been a strategic decision by the management.

The branch was struggling as it could not meet its targets in deposits and loans – they needed someone to turn it around. They found no-one like Sheshadri to do so. It was a move he also had wanted, bringing him closer to his hometown.

Within a year, he had transformed the branch. Targets were being met, the branch was thriving, and Sheshu's reputation soared. He was promoted to Assistant General Manager, but the management kept him at Broadway by raising the branch to AGM level – that huge was his impact there. By the second year, his branch was a model for others. After that, the branch met targets regularly not just in deposits and loans, but in NRI deposits as well. The management would advise other managers to emulate the splendid work being done by Sheshadri.

But then, everything came crashing down. It started with a phone call.

The voice on the other end belonged to Sahasranamam, the General Manager of the Legal Cell at Head Office.

"Sheshadri," he had said, his tone a mix of disbelief and concern. "What's going on? How could you make such a mistake? The loan you sanctioned for Cherai Beach House – it's against rules."

"What do you mean?" Sheshu had asked, his heart sinking.

"I'm looking at the documents you submitted. There's no proper title deed for the entire eighty acres. And do you realise it falls under the Coastal Zone Regulation Act? Everything built there is illegal. Sheshadri, this loan – forty crores – might as well be thrown into the sea."

When Sahasranamam spoke, Seshadri froze.

That wasn't a mistake he'd ever imagined himself making. Maybe it was an error born of the desperation to meet loan targets. Feeling like a child caught red-handed, he blurted out,

"What do we do now?"

For a moment, there was silence at the other end. Then Sahasranamam, his voice measured but cautious, replied, "Since this loan hasn't been officially approved by the head office, the entire responsibility falls on you. So, you'll need to recover the full amount, including interest, in one go."

Seshadri's heart sank. He asked in a low voice, "Is that even possible?"

The reply came, sharp and unforgiving: "It has to be. Otherwise, the case will look like the manager colluded with some fraudsters to syphon off forty crores from the bank. And you know how these things go – the same people who held you up yesterday will throw you under the bus tomorrow. This banking job is a thankless grind."

The words felt like a noose tightening around him.

Seshadri left the branch immediately, not telling anyone where he was going. He drove to the beach house, praying desperately all the way for a miracle. But his prayers went unanswered.

The beach house had been presented as a future tourist haven, an international-class resort. But Sahadevan, the entrepreneur who had taken the loan, had channelled every rupee into the land purchase. There was no money left for development, and the deserted beach house wasn't bringing in a single *paisa* of income. Worse, the property had legal issues, and the documents were not in order. Selling it to recover the loan wasn't even an option.

Despair clawed at Seshadri. He turned to threats.

"If the money isn't repaid," he told Sahadevan, "it won't just be me going to jail for defrauding the bank – you'll be there too."

That night, Seshadri didn't sleep. He sat up, his mind racing in circles, praying over and over, "God, show me a way."

When morning came, he returned to the bank, exhausted and defeated. But the moment he walked in, he saw a man waiting for him – a man in spotless white clothes. When he met him and heard his instructions, he understood that his prayers had been answered.

Without any introductions or pleasantries, the man spoke: "Swami, my name is Yusuf Khan. I'm in the real estate business. I've heard about the Cherayi Beach House. I'm willing to take it over."

Seshadri stared at him, unsure if he was hearing correctly. Khan continued and Seshu felt he was listening to a benevolent God.

"I know about the issues with the title deeds. There are even lands without *pattas*. I also understand that the government could demolish the property at any time as they were built in violation of CRZ rules. Even so, I'm ready to repay the full loan amount, with interest. And I'll make sure the owner gets a fair price."

Seshadri felt a weight lifted off his chest. He couldn't find the words to express his relief. Khan's next question brought him back to reality.

"How do you want the payment – cash, draft, or cheque?"

Overwhelmed, Seshadri stammered,

"Mr Yusuf Khan, you've come at a time when I needed a miracle to get out of a huge crisis. Since you're willing to take over the property knowing well all its issues, I'll speak with the owner and figure out the payment process."

Khan nodded but made one condition clear: "I'll pay the money. But I want the beach house and every inch of land tied to it – whether documented or not. That's where your role as the manager comes in."

At that moment, Seshadri didn't care about conditions or challenges. He was willing to do whatever it took to resolve the situation.

When he approached the property owner with Khan's proposal, the man refused flatly.

"Let the bank take legal action. We'll deal with it," he said, defiant.

Seshadri was back to square one. But once again, Khan had a solution.

"Swami, you just need to sit in the car as the manager. Leave the rest to me. I'll take care of it," Yusuf Khan had said.

When they headed out that night to the beach house owner's residence, four government vehicles followed them.

As Sheshadri sat in the car, unsure of what was happening, Khan explained calmly: "Those vehicles? They're carrying officers from the CBI's financial crimes division, a Reserve Bank team investigating bank fraud, your bank's senior officials, and top brass from the state revenue department. I won't step out. All you have to do, Swami, is stand with them quietly. Rest assured, it will be done."

Sheshadri felt his heart race with fear.

Sensing his trepidation, Khan reassured him. "Don't worry. They're all my people. The matter will go exactly as planned."

When Sheshadri stepped out with the group of officials, the beach house owner looked visibly shaken.

The team began without preamble, stating, "We've uncovered the state's biggest banking fraud."

They continued, pointing to Swami, "Here's the manager, already in custody." Then turning to the owner, they delivered the next blow. "You're under arrest as well. You've embezzled forty crores by making him a scapegoat, and we're here to take you to Bombay."

The owner, initially defiant, demanded to call his lawyer and partners. But as the reality of the situation sank in, he began pleading: "I'll pay back the bank, even if it means selling my property. Just let me go."

One of the officials replied coldly, "If you'd sorted this out before we arrived, we could've helped. But now, it's out of our hands."

After some deliberation among themselves, they laid out an option. "Can you repay the amount in full right now? If the bank gets its money, there won't be a case. We can leave, and our job here will be done."

Desperate, the owner stammered, "How am I supposed to arrange that kind of money tonight?"

But the officials weren't letting up.

"If you really want to, it's possible. Isn't there a land bank here? If you provide the consent letter and the land documents, any land bank will pay you immediately." Then, turning to Sheshadri, they asked, "If the money is arranged, can the bank release the documents?"

Sheshadri nodded.

The owner hesitated, admitting he didn't know any local land banks.

An official stepped in to help.

Within half an hour, a representative from Hindustan Land Bank arrived, ready with stamp papers. A sales deed was drawn up, and the beach house owner signed it reluctantly.

The officials handed over a cheque for forty-three crore

rupees, including interest, to Sheshadri. As he looked at the cheque, it dawned on him – it was from the NRI account of Takiyuddin, a customer of his bank. The account had sufficient funds to honour the cheque.

That's how Sheshadri found himself getting closer to Yusuf Khan. Khan suggested a unique approach for resolving the bank's liabilities: if there were similar pledged properties in coastal areas, they could be acquired. It wasn't about fraud or deceit – the properties were bought at a fair price, ensuring no loss to the owners.

Sheshadri's bank had seven long-standing non-performing loans, five of which were tied to properties in coastal regions. Among them were two ice plants, a coir unit, and two fish-processing factories. Under Khan's plan, these properties were sold at reasonable rates, clearing the loans owed to the bank, and Hindustan Land Bank acquired them.

The management showered Sheshadri with praise for recovering not just the forty crores the bank had written off, but also other bad debts deemed irrecoverable. But this time, the recognition didn't touch him.

The very system that had turned its back on him when he made an inadvertent mistake was now trying to pull him close again.

Sheshadri realised that banking was a thankless job – just as Sahasranamam had said. He started to think about leaving the bank at the right moment.

It was during this phase of reflection that Yusuf Khan showed up at the bank one day, unexpectedly. Amid a casual conversation, Khan suddenly asked, "Swami, how much do you earn?"

Sheshadri was surprised by the question. "Why do you ask, Khan?" he asked, curious.

Khan smiled. "Looking at the responsibilities you shoulder and the skill you bring to your job, I couldn't help but wonder."

"Well," Sheshadri replied, "around forty thousand... and with allowances and benefits, it comes up to fifty thousand."

Khan chuckled and then spoke with seriousness. "I'll pay you two *lakhs* a month. Sixty thousand on paper and a hundred and forty in black. On top of that, you'll get a car, a house, a phone, and other benefits. What do you say – are you coming with me?"

Sheshadri laughed, assuming Khan wasn't serious. "What's the job?" he asked. "Regional Manager of the Land Bank," Khan replied.

Sheshadri looked puzzled. "I don't quite understand."

"We run a chain of land banks," Khan explained. "Instead of handling money, we deal in land. Your job would be simple – just like this, identify pledged properties tied to liabilities in other banks. Acquire them. Once that's done, we'll look at other opportunities."

Still baffled, Sheshadri remained silent.

Khan, sensing his confusion, elaborated further. "All the land in this region is coming under our control. Imagine a future where no-one but us has claims over this soil. When people need land, they'll come to us. And we'll sell it only to those we choose."

Sheshadri listened intently, drawn in by the novelty and daring of the idea. Perhaps it was his frustration with the traps of his current job or the realisation that there would be no-one to save him if things went wrong that made Khan's offer seem compelling.

"Life needs some thrill, Swami," Khan continued, reading his thoughts. "Not just life – your job should have some excitement too. Take VRS (voluntary retirement scheme) from the bank. Invest the amount you get in something secure and come with me. I'll deposit five years' worth of your salary in a bank account, and I'll give you cheques so that you can withdraw it monthly. Isn't that a good enough guarantee?"

Sheshadri had initially been listening out of curiosity, but

Khan's words began to take root in his mind. Finally, he said, "Let me think about it."

That evening, as Sheshadri walked home, his mind was racing. One thing stood out: he needed to discuss this with Venkateshwaran.

Venkateshwaran was a clerk in the census office in Thiruvananthapuram. He visited every Saturday night and left early Monday morning, so there was only one day in a week they could meet. Despite being mired in his own struggles, Venkateshwaran had a knack for offering sound advice that benefited others. Sheshadri often admired him for that.

Venkateshwaran's family home was a small three-room house on First Puthentheruvu Street. He had sold it to Kichamani, a pickle merchant, to fund his two sisters' weddings. Now, he lived there as a tenant. His dream was to buy three cents of land near the village and build a small house for his family.

On weekends, he would gather his wife and two children to excitedly describe the land he intended to buy and the house he planned to build. When they were alone, Venki would confide in Sheshadri:

"I don't think I'll ever be able to buy those three cents or build that house in my lifetime. Only I know how hard it is to make ends meet on my salary."

Half-seriously, half-jokingly, he'd add, "You're my only hope, Sheshu. You don't have a family or other burdens. Buy me those three cents of land. Once my kids finish their studies, get jobs and settle down, I'll repay you every *paisa*."

Sheshadri had taken that request seriously and had promised, "Venki, you look for the land. I'll buy it for you."

But Venkateshwaran always brushed it off, saying, "Not now. When you buy land for Rudrabhoomi, you can get me a plot nearby."

I held back from asking how Venki knew about Rudrabhoomi, a secret known only to me. By the time I thought of asking, Sheshu had already begun recounting the incident:

During Anantha Shastri's final moments, both Sheshu and Venki were by his side. His last words were: "When I die, they'll take me to the electric crematorium. I dread the thought of it. No-one from our street should ever face such a fate. If no-one else helps, you must do it on your own – a crematorium of our own. The Rudrabhoomi of our dreams."

Venki had also heard Appa's last words.

As Sheshu recounted this, his eyes were filled with tears. He gazed silently into the distance for a while, lost in thought. Then, wiping his eyes with the back of his hand, he said:

"That was a Saturday, so Venki was at the bhajan hall in the community centre. From the Cherai Beach House issue to my most recent conversation with Yusuf Khan, I narrated everything to him. After hearing it all, Venki asked me a few pointed questions: 'Are you sure you absolutely need the bank job? Do you really believe you'll be given five years' salary from the Land Bank?'

"Answering him wasn't difficult. Eventually, I told him, 'Honestly, after what happened in Cherai, I'm done with the bank job. The Land Bank will deposit five years' worth of salary in advance under my name and issue me cheques for the same.'

"Venki spoke next, with a vision for the future: 'You have to survive, don't you? Use the interest from the VRS amount for that. With three years' worth of salary from the land bank, we can create Rudrabhoomi.'

"At one point, I joked, 'Don't we need to buy your three cents of land too?' and Venki replied seriously, 'You'll have to think everything through carefully...'

"There wasn't much to think about. I opted for VRS from the bank, and before officially joining hands with Yusuf Khan, money worth the five years' of salary he promised was deposited in my name, and Khan handed over to me monthly cheques in one go, saying: 'Swami, you can set up an office wherever you prefer, buy any car you like – even your personal expenses, including a phone, are no issue. To put it simply, money isn't a problem.'

"I set up the office at Marine Drive and got the car I wanted. Khan even stocked the office with a substantial amount of cash, making it clear there were no spending limits. Within a month, I acquired twenty-nine properties – set aside for securitisation – across seventeen banks in the city for Hindustan Land Bank. Before the auction processes began, I negotiated directly with the owners, paid them the agreed amount, and ensured the registration was completed after settling the bank dues.

"Khan never interfered in pricing or additional payouts to owners. Whenever I explained the deals as a prelude to seeking approval, his response was always the same: 'Consider it all yours, Swami, and proceed accordingly.'

"However, Khan was very strict about one condition in financial transactions – the amounts mentioned in the property deeds had to match the cheques issued. For this, cheques were drawn from the foreign investments of three NRI directors of Hindustan Land Bank: Takkiyuddin, Mohiyuddin, and Badruddin. These directors ensured the cheques aligned with official amounts, while any off-the-record cash payments were delivered promptly within a maximum of three hours – whether in wads of thousand- or five-hundred-rupee notes. All new notes!

"Once, for a deal in Vallarpadam, I needed to pay ₹7.5 crore in cash in addition to the cheque to the landowner who refused to step out of his house for registration without upfront payment. When I informed Khan over the phone, his response was immediate: 'Stay there, Swami. The money will arrive on-site.'

"Within an hour, a thin man who looked like a fabric merchant arrived rowing a boat, carrying a cloth bundle.

Without saying a word, he handed it over and left. When I opened it, it contained ₹7.5 crore.

"When I mentioned these massive unaccounted cash dealings to Venki, he cautioned me to watch out for counterfeit notes. I reassured him, saying, 'I've handled currency for thirty years – I can identify fakes just by touch.' Even so, as a precaution, I used a fake note detector and searchlight to double check the currency Khan provided. Not once did I find a counterfeit.

"In just six months, I acquired most of the properties marked for auction due to defaulted loans from banks. That's when Khan said: 'You've completed in six months what was meant to take five years. Because of this, the company's directors are extremely pleased with you. Keep up the pace and acquire as much land as possible. Price is not an issue – that's the directors' stance.'

"At that point, I asked Khan: 'I haven't met any of the directors yet. Why is that?' Khan's response was quick: 'They're all based abroad. They've given me the power of attorney to handle all operations here as the Chief Executive. Just as you oversee the Central Region, we have managers for the north and south regions, along with zonal and area-level teams. They all follow the same instructions.' After a pause, Khan added, 'The directors evaluate the performance of all regions and zones daily. Swami, you're the best.'

"Khan's words had a certain intoxicating effect on me – motivating me to carry out at least one transaction every week. Every deal required giving proper 'cuts' to local thugs, brokers, and officials – including the police. Most of the time, local politicians decided the payoffs, and Khan instructed me to comply without causing friction. This made all transactions smooth.

"When I had acquired properties worth ₹3,000 crore for Hindustan Land Bank, Khan said: 'We now have 37 designated land banks under Hindustan Land Bank, as per our initial plan. Kerala Land Bank requires land in South Kochi,

Cochin Land Bank in West Kochi, Bharatmata Land Bank in Panangad-Maradu-Vyttila Bypass, and Kakkanad Land Bank around the proposed Smart City area. Within Ernakulam city, it's Rishinagakkulam Land Bank's responsibility.'

"That's when I interrupted: 'Why is one of the land banks called Rishinagakkulam? Is it named after a director's family?" Khan proudly replied: 'That's Ernakulam's old name. All our land banks have names that evoke national or regional sentiments. It was a specific directive from the directors.'

"I didn't say much after that. I focused on gathering records of ownership for lands in those areas from village, taluk, and registration offices. I offered whatever price they demanded for registration. Most were willing to sell when offered lucrative deals. A few sought time to reconsider, while others outright refused. For those who resisted, we had special tactics. For instance, Wilson Paulose, who refused to sell one and a half acres in Maradu, was trapped in a sexual harassment case. The investigating DySP acted as a mediator and ultimately facilitated the purchase.

"Similarly, VR Pisharadi, who obtained a stay order against selling his property on Central Road, withdrew the stay after his daughter went missing. It was only after she called from an unknown location that the deal went through.

"Another incident revolved around a property belonging to Panangattu Madhava Menon. Although Menon was willing to sell the land, his unmarried younger brother opposed the decision, claiming a stake in it. Tragically, the brother died in a car accident, which paved the way for a smooth transaction. While the disappearance of obstacles was convenient, it also instilled a deep sense of unease and fear. When I shared these concerns with Yusuf Khan, he dismissed them with a casual, 'We don't need to worry about such things. Let's just focus on the job.'

"Within a year, we had acquired land worth ₹7,000 crore in the designated areas. That's when Khan remarked: 'This time, you lagged a bit behind. Across the south and north regions, we've already purchased land worth ₹17,000 crore through twenty different land banks.' Perhaps sensing my disappointment, he continued: 'Don't worry. We've got some special assignments in the Central region this time. If we complete those, Swami, you will surely rise to the top.'

"In response to this, I asked: 'What kind of assignments?' To which Khan replied: 'I'm not sure. Our Country Head is arriving tomorrow. He'll explain everything.' I was confused by this development. 'Who is the Country Head?' I asked. 'I've never heard of him.' Khan, with his usual air of mystery, said, 'His name is Ali Ahmad Nijad. I haven't met him in person yet, but we speak regularly over the phone.'

"This, however, wasn't enough for me. I pressed Khan for more: 'Where does he live? Where's his office?' But Khan, still maintaining his enigmatic demeanour, simply replied, 'They're all bigshots. Do you think we'd know such things?'

"'But shouldn't we know about him, at least to some extent?' I insisted. 'We'll meet him tomorrow. You can ask him yourself,' he replied evasively.

"The meeting with the Country Head was arranged aboard a luxury yacht, four nautical miles off the Kochi coast. To reach the yacht, we took a boat from a private jetty on an island. During the boat ride, Khan introduced me to the regional managers. N. Vasudeva Sharma, the head of the southern region, was a retired Superintendent of Police from a prominent Namboothiri family with a communist legacy in southern Travancore. P.K.K. Menon, the northern region head, was a former Deputy Collector from a renowned aristocratic family in Ottapalam. Khan clarified that representatives from the zonal region weren't invited to this meeting.

"Despite being called a luxury yacht, it was more like a mid-sized ship. Onboard were Sharma, Menon, Khan, and me. Nijad himself was on the deck to welcome us. His greeting, delivered in impeccable English with an Oxford accent, was both gracious and commanding: 'I extend a warm welcome to you, the accomplished individuals driving this noble mission forward. Although I am referred to as the Country Head, the responsibility for this nation doesn't lie solely with me. There are others like me, but as far as you are concerned, I am the go-to person. Please enjoy my hospitality as you see fit. Afterward, each of you will have a one-on-one meeting with me, lasting an hour.'

"After a brief formal introduction, Nijad retreated into the inner chambers of the ship. The vessel, in the middle of the sea, felt like a floating paradise. Alcohol flowed freely, complemented by exquisite food and the company of eight stunning Lebanese beauties, willing to go the extra mile.

"After everything, the meeting with Nijad took place sometime very late in the night. During my one-hour private meeting, he pointed to areas in the map and lithophane of Ernakulam district where the glow of fluorescent highlighters and said: 'These unmarked areas are not ours yet. We need continuity of land, so we must acquire them all, especially the plots between Maradu and the island. If we purchase those twelve plots, we'll own all the land between the sea and the bypass. We must buy it, no matter the cost.'

"'I've tried, but they won't sell,' I replied.

"Pointing to another section on the lithoplan, Nijad said: 'If we buy these 74 acres, currently divided into four parts, we'll eliminate any possibility of competition in that area.'

"I explained that the land was of little use, being merely a coastal strip restricted by the Coastal Zone Regulation Act, making any development impossible. Nijad's response was unwavering: 'We don't need it for development – we need it for control. No-one else should have a claim to this land.'

"His tone softened slightly as he transitioned to the next set of instructions. 'Around the airport, there are several parcels of land owned by seventeen people. Those must be bought. Price should not be a constraint. Similarly, near the railway station and the port, there are strategic areas we need to acquire. All of it is marked here.'

"When I admitted I hadn't considered some of these areas, Nijad was firm: 'Start now and secure them.' He paused for a moment as if gathering his thoughts, then added, 'In Ernakulam district, these are the critical purchases. Beyond that, you're free to buy land wherever you find opportunities. But I have a personal preference: the coastal areas and isolated islands must entirely belong to us. It's not just about business – it's about an emotional connection to the land.'

"His passion for land acquisition was evident, leaving me both amazed and slightly unnerved. Sensing my unease, Nijad continued: 'I'm not giving you too many targets. The four tasks I've assigned are non-negotiable. After that, do as much as you can.'

"When it was time to leave, Nijad's words carried a strange blend of kindness and resolve. 'We'll meet again. You're more capable than I had expected,' he said, with a faint smile. He then gave me the option to either stay aboard the yacht for the night or return to shore. After passing on these choices, Nijad summoned Sharma and Menon, instructing them: 'Give me one hour each for private discussions.'

"Despite the Lebanese hostesses' insistence, I didn't feel inclined to stay aboard the yacht. Instead, I returned alone.

"Once back onshore, I threw myself into work with renewed energy. We successfully acquired most of the properties Nijad had pointed out. In Bolgatty, a deal that initially stalled due to opposition from Dineshan, a leader of the local environmental protection committee, gained momentum after his mysterious disappearance. Dineshan's body was later found in the backwaters of Kochi, sparking a flurry of rumours.

"Similarly, in Kakkanad, the opposition to two major properties was fierce. Yet, for reasons unknown, those opposing the deal turned into allies within days, facilitating the transactions. Some speculated that threats, blackmail, money, or even women might have played a role, but nothing was certain.

"From phone conversations with Sharma and Menon, I

realised that similar progress was being made in the other two regions. Menon concentrated on coastal areas in Kasaragod, Kannur, Kozhikode, and Thrissur. Sharma, meanwhile, targeted both coastal zones and large-scale developments in Thiruvananthapuram, Kollam, and Alappuzha. Overseeing it all was Yusuf Khan. At times, I felt compelled to ask him what was really happening. One day, I finally mustered the courage to question him. Without hesitation, he revealed the details:

"'Nijad has given us one more target: Kundannoor's First Puthen Street. If we can acquire it, everything to the west of the bypass will belong entirely to the company. This includes three ponds and two temples with spacious courtyards. One of the temples is dedicated to Goddess Bhuvaneswari. Nijad has instructed us to establish a company named Bhuvaneswari Land Developers and begin operations there.

"I stood silent for a moment, unsure of how to respond. This was the street where I was born and raised. It was the soil where I had played as a child, the earth imprinted with the footsteps of my parents. The thought of acquiring it for someone else felt unbearable.

"As I struggled to find the words, Yusuf Khan spoke again: 'Nijad asked me to inform you about this and have directed me to call them once you're briefed. He'll explain how to proceed.' Even as he was speaking, Khan dialled Nijad on his mobile and handed the phone to me.

"What followed wasn't a request – it was an order from Nijad: 'Swami is well-respected in Kundannoor, you should go there today itself.' He then laid out the instructions clearly:

"There are 49 houses on First Puthen Street that need to be acquired. Give them enough time to vacate, but ensure that the registration of sale deed is completed as quickly as possible. Pay the price they demand. For those who need homes, offer them houses in Kalpathy or Mylapore. For those seeking jobs, provide opportunities in Chennai or Bangalore. If anyone refuses to vacate willingly, report it to me. Nijad didn't wait for my response.

"It had been a long time since I visited Kundannoor. The reasons were many –primarily the workload. After exhausting days, I would usually stay in a city hotel. Several premium hotels always kept four or five rooms blocked for our use. Moreover, I often wondered, whom would I visit back home? Most of the families had moved on. If Venki had been around, I would have gone without hesitation. But he had been in Kolkata for a while, staying with his younger sister's family. Her husband was battling terminal cancer, and Venki had taken an unpaid leave to support them.

"After much deliberation, I decided to carry out the new assignment. The first house I approached belonged to Gopalaswamy. When I explained the situation, Swamy seemed pleased, but he demanded a hefty price – one unheard of in the area. His son and daughter-in-law were both employed at an IT company in Chennai. Swamy was willing to sell his seven-cent house in the village if he could get an apartment in Mylapore and ₹25 lakhs: 'And anyway, isn't it for a project in the name of Bhuvaneswari? At least let the temple flourish,' he added, almost theatrically.

"The neighbouring house belonged to Veeramani Iyer, who was also willing to sell. However, he insisted that the buyer must be a Brahmin. My arrival seemed to make him happy. In return, he asked for a house his sister had put up for sale in Kalpathy, along with ₹30 lakhs.

"Of the forty-nine houses, one belonged to me, and another was rented out to Venki. Of the remaining forty-seven, thirty families were ready to vacate for a fair price. The rest – seventeen families – refused. When I informed Nijad about this, he seemed pleased: 'Complete the registration for the willing sellers quickly. The rest will sell within a month,' he said confidently.

"Despite my efforts, I couldn't figure out how that would happen. Nonetheless, we registered the properties of the willing families. Some even requested additional time to stay in their homes, which we happily granted. However, Yusuf Khan allowed outsiders to move into the vacated houses.

"Complaints began to surface. One such newcomer allegedly entered Maniswami's bedroom, prompting Swamy to vacate. Another incident involved an attempted rape on Vishwanatha Iyer's daughter. Narayanamoorthy's legs were broken by someone, and there was an attempt to murder Krishna Iyer. A widow named Gomathi Ammal found fish strewn in her prayer room. With such incidents piling up, most villagers eventually sold their homes, and even the reluctant ones began to consider selling off.

"It was during this phase that Venki returned from Kolkata. Sitting on the steps of his rented house, he asked me in a voice filled with anguish: 'Sheshu, to whom are you selling all our land? Where will we, rootless people, go now? Our forefathers, our temples, our gods... To whom have you sold them? Where will we establish our Rudrabhoomi?' He paused, looked at my face, and asked again: 'You had once told me you would help me buy three cents of land here. Get me that land now... I am not leaving this place. This is my land...'

"I did not take Venki's fervent plea and emotional outburst seriously. Bolstered by the funds I had at my disposal, I reassured him: 'I have the money to build a burial ground. I will buy you land and also build a house on it.'

"Hearing this, he laughed like a madman. 'Once everyone leaves this place, for whom will your burial ground be? When all the houses and lands in this street are sold, where will you find land for me?'

"Faced with these questions, I was shaken. I could not stay there any longer. I immediately sought Yusuf Khan and told him: 'I need to meet our country head today itself.' Khan assured me after listening: 'I am not sure if he is on land or at sea – in any case, arrangements can be made by tonight.'

"As usual, the meeting was on a pleasure yacht on the open

sea. Uncharacteristically, he came down to the lower platform. Nijad's looked very stern, devoid of any pleasantries. Before I could say anything, his voice, imbued with gravity, resonated: 'A mature businessman cannot afford sentiments. A man who sees a goat, if he's a poet, will adore it. A shepherd will assess how much milk it can give. But a butcher, a businessman like me, will measure its weight – for the meat it can yield. Swamy and I belong to the third category. Forget whatever that Venki said.'

"I couldn't contain myself: 'That's not something one can just forget. First Puthen Street is the land where we were born and raised. We have a dream there. It cannot be forgotten.'

"Nijad laughed: 'I must own that land... everything beyond and beneath that is mine. Outsiders in between will be inconvenient.' When I started to argue again, Nijad's tone changed. 'Do you know why I anchor here in this sea? To take in everything I dislike, I need the sea. When you conducted land deals, did anyone oppose you, Swami? Those who couldn't be tempted or intimidated were swallowed by this sea. If I now put you through the grinder alive and mix your mashed body with the sea water, even the smallest fish will find it a delicacy.'

"Though Nijad spoke in a low voice, its undertones carried an electric current that I could feel: 'Swami, please leave. Venki will not come again to change Swami's mind." He paused and continued: 'We never had this meeting, understood? If you have any plans to be a whistleblower, just know that I will bring Swami back here myself...'"When I started to argue again, Nijad, visibly uneasy, interrupted: 'I don't have the time to handle you now. I have some very important guests today...' Saying this, he grabbed my hand and took me to the deck. Standing just outside the buzzing deck, Nijad pointed toward a group and asked: 'Do you see those VIPs enjoying themselves there?'

"I clearly recognised them – a small group that included Sahasranamam, the General Manager of the State Bank and my former boss. Many other faces were familiar – three political leaders who epitomised ideals, a beloved movie star, and notable officials. There were also power brokers, senior police officers, notorious gang leaders, and underworld figures. I froze, unable to process the unexpected sight.

"Noticing my expression, Nijad asked: 'Do you think Swami can escape from these people, who'd do anything for me, even if I let you go?' Before I could respond, Nijad issued a firm order: 'Stop wasting time. Go now. Be an obedient boy and finish the job.'

"I wanted to say something, but I didn't know what. My better judgment kept me silent.

"As I returned to the shore, my thoughts were consumed by Venki. Nijad's words, 'Venki won't come back to change Swami's mind,' echoed ominously. Was it a warning? My gut told him it was. Could I continue working for someone like Nijad? That was a question I could no longer avoid. At the very least, I decided it would be wise to take precautions. I needed to reach my office quickly, retrieve critical documents and personal funds. Money was essential. At any cost, I had to buy Venki a house and some land.

"The moment I arrived at the shore, I made a beeline for the office. As I was stepping inside, the attendant spoke up: 'Sir, someone has been waiting for quite some time... I allowed him to stay even though it was late, as he insisted it was urgent...'

"I asked who it was, to which the attendant replied: 'He says he's a broker. His name's Balu.'

"I nodded. This seemed like someone I could trust with finding Venki a house near the village. Offering him a commission of two percent, along with an extra one percent, should get him to quickly find both the land and the house. I said: 'Tell him to come in. Quickly.'

"The person waiting outside walked in. To my surprise though, it was a broker I didn't recognise. Before we could exchange pleasantries, I spoke first: 'Mr Balu, I need you to find a house and some land for me today. Anywhere near

Kundannur First Puthan Street is fine. Price isn't an issue…
I'll pay you an extra one percent brokerage.'

"For a brief moment, the man seemed taken aback. Then,
with a hint of hesitation, he replied: 'I'm not actually a
broker. I told the attendant I was, just to get inside.' I raised
an eyebrow, my irritation showing. 'Who are you then? What
do you want?'

"The stranger broke into a smile, his eyes twinkling with
recognition: 'Look at me properly, Seshadri, and then tell
me if you remember me.'"If this person had gone to such
lengths to enter my office, he must be someone important.
My gaze sharpened, studying the man closely, but no flash of
recognition came. Sensing my confusion, the stranger added:
'You must have forgotten me, huh? We were schoolmates.
I'm Balu. Balasubrahmanyam!'

"The words hit like a bolt. Balasubrahmanyam – my old
schoolmate, the youngest member of our old school group,
the son of Professor Seshagopalan who used to live behind
the community hall. His family had left Kundannur when his
father was transferred to another engineering college and I
hadn't heard from him since. Venki had once spoken of him,
mentioning he was sharp and had topped at IIT Madras.

"Still in disbelief, I stood up and walked over to Balu,
placing a hand on his shoulder, my voice a mixture of
astonishment and warmth: 'I can't believe this… after all
these years, how is it that we never crossed paths again? I
even heard you were at IIT Madras. And now, where have
you been? Family? Kids?'"Balu paused for a moment, his
expression shifting into something more serious. He closed
his eyes and spoke slowly: 'Seshadri, I'm not here for the
reasons you might think… I've come for something specific
today…'

"My heart skipped a beat. Sensing there was something
important coming, I asked, 'What is it?'

"Balu opened his eyes. There was an unmistakable gleam
in them – two stars burning brightly. It felt as though his voice

emanated from the very depths of those eyes. 'Who owns your land bank, Seshadri? Where does he live?'Though the question came as a surprise, I quickly responded: 'It's nothing much. This is a project by the National Land Developers Company. The company has three directors...' Before I could finish, though, Balu expressed discomfort.

"He said: 'I know. The three NRIs, including Thakkiyudheen, are just names thrown up to collect and distribute money. But do you know who the real owner is, Seshadri? Where does he live? I need to know...'

"I responded: 'I've told you what I know. Our Chief Executive, Yusuf Khan, would know better.' As I showed my helplessness, however, Balu continued. He said: 'Yusuf Khan is just another worker like you! I need to know who is the real owner and his headquarters – or at least a way to reach him...'

"Hearing this, I felt a cold unfamiliarity creeping in. And as Balu pressed on with his questions, I began to feel truly uneasy. 'Balu Subrahmanyam,' I began, 'what are you really after? Who are you, really?' When Balu didn't answer immediately, I asked again. 'Are there any illegal activities going on in this business? If so, you must tell me. I need to remove myself from this.'

"Balu smiled calmly. 'Seshadri, don't panic – if you promise not to let anyone know about me or our conversation I will reveal everything to you.' He paused for a moment and then continued with quiet resolve. 'The word of Ananthashastrigal's son is enough for me – I know the Seshadri I remember can't break his word.'

"'And so, I gave him my word. It was not just any promise, but an oath taken with the spirit of my father and the divine Bhuvaneswari as witnesses. It was only after this moment that Balu's words struck me with shocking clarity. You see, Balu Subrahmanyam was a Maoist activist, having joined the movement while studying at IIT Madras. He spent seven years in Nepal, and after completing his training there, he was sent to South India. He began in Andhra Pradesh, then moved to

Karnataka, and later to Tamil Nadu. In Tamil Nadu villages, where caste hierarchy reigned supreme, Balasubrahmanyam managed to establish strong roots for the Maoist party.

"After a police encounter in Periyakulam, where several comrades were killed, he crossed into Kerala through Poonchiyar, near the Parambikulam border. He set up camps in Pala, Karamada, Anakkatti, Palamalai, Uliyur, Mulliyar, and Attikadavu, to train operatives. It was during this time that he was instructed to pose as a labour supervisor among construction workers from Bihar and Bengal who had come to Kerala.

"Balu explained: 'Our primary target here is the land mafia,' he said, his voice steady and resolute. 'In the beginning, we didn't view Kerala the same way we saw other states,' he continued. 'Kerala traditionally didn't have large-scale feudal landlords. That was mainly because of the land reform laws introduced by the first communist government. There were also efforts to restore alienated tribal lands. But all of that has now been overturned. The land mafia has established dominance here.

"He took a breath and continued: 'In places like Munnar, Vagamon, Kumarakom, and Kovalam, they're grabbing land under the guise of tourism. In other areas, like Lower Kuttanad, Kerala's rice bowl, their invasion is backed by hawala money. Some of the political leaders here act as their middlemen or even their enforcers. They deceive the poor, taking over their lands with empty promises. They're buying up huge tracts of land near upcoming project zones, forcing the locals out before the plans are even announced.'

"Balu's voice grew more impassioned as he spoke. 'The ordinary people here have become the prey, unable to recognise the hunters. At a time when those who should protect them have turned into their oppressors, our mission is to confront the land mafia and secure the land for the common people. We need your help to identify the invaders who are displacing the poor from their own soil.'

"Balu's words and tone had the weight of a speech. Perhaps that's why I asked, half-mockingly, 'So, what exactly do you want me to do?'

"'Give us the details about the land's true owner,' Balu replied directly.

"I finished his response with finality: 'I've told you everything I know.'

"'No,' Balu countered firmly. 'You know more than that.'

"I shook my head. 'I only know about those who pay my salary – I've already said as much.'

"Hearing this, Balu's voice took on a sharp edge. 'Is this coming from the son of Ananthasasthri, the early communist who divided his family's land in Kundannoor and gave it away to the community members long before Kerala's land reforms? You, of all people, should be standing with us to destroy the land mafia.'

"Balu's words made me uncomfortable. 'I have a job now... I get paid. Political and social activism isn't on my agenda,' I retorted.

"Balu responded patiently, though his tone carried an unyielding conviction. 'This isn't about politics – this is now a matter of public interest. The land we reclaimed from landlords through land reforms is falling into the hands of the new landlords – the land mafia. They'll sell this land to anyone who pays, perhaps even to enemy nations! Who knows if enemy nations are behind these purchases? Or worse, if they aren't being made to buy this land for enemy nations' purposes! That's why we must find the source of this land mafia and uproot it completely.' Balu paused for a moment before continuing, his voice firm: 'If you ever change your mind, let me know. I'll be at the Paradise Complex worksite on Grant Road, working as a labourer.'

"As Balu Subrahmanyam walked away, for some reason, Venki's face flashed in my mind. Without thinking, I rushed to First Puthen Street.

"When I reached Venki's rented house, I noticed a small

crowd gathered in front. My heart sank. Approaching the yard, I noticed a white sheet covering someone lying on the ground. Venki's wife and children were wailing nearby. Someone spoke, their voice flat: 'He suffocated in his sleep... there was no struggle or suffering. A peaceful death.'

"Venki's wife stopped crying abruptly and turned to me, her eyes wide. Then, Venki's brother-in-law, Subbaraman, leaned in and whispered in my ear: 'Come outside for a moment – I need to tell you something.'

"Still in shock, I followed Subbaraman outside. Once we were away from the others, Subbaraman spoke in a hushed voice, trembling with fear: 'I came here to see my sister. There was no space inside, so Venki and I were sleeping outside. Venki on the cot, and I on the ground. During the night, I saw two people come and smother Venki's face. Even though I heard the struggle, I didn't move out of fear for my life. After making sure he was dead, they ran away. It was only then that I went to Venki's side. Even then, he wasn't dead. Hearing the commotion, she and the children woke up and came out. Venki, gasping for breath, muttered to me: 'You must tell Sheshu...' The family couldn't understand what it was. Then, from under the pillow, he handed this to me.'

"Sheshadri lifted the piece of metal from around his neck and told me: 'This is the piece of metal that Subbaraman had extended that day. Poor Venki was carrying it around as a model for Rudrabhoomi's nameboard...'

"When Subbaraman received the model of the nameboard to be placed in front of the intended crematorium, Venki had told him: 'Before you bury me, you must hand this over to Sheshu.'

"Later, Subbaraman spoke apologetically. He was scared of the police. If it was found to be a murder, the police would arrive, a post-mortem would be required, and the family would be disgraced. That's why he didn't tell the truth even to his sister: 'Everyone believes that Venki's death was due to a heart attack in his sleep. Let it remain that way.'

"At that moment, I felt I should wear the metal piece engraved with the word Rudrabhoomi around my own neck. The experience of having my dear Venki hanging from my neck, close to my chest! Venki whispered to my heart: 'Where is my Rudrabhoomi? The beautiful crematorium you promised for the dead and those yet to die – where is it?'

"I felt as though my heart was breaking. 'Venki will not come anymore to change Swami's mind,' Nijad had declared. And within hours, he took Venki's life! Sheshadri felt an overwhelming anger against Nijad. What crime did Venki commit to deserve the death penalty?

"Without even stepping inside to pay respects to the corpse, I ran out. At that moment, my mind had only one goal – Nijad! And the only solution – Balasubrahmanyam!

"Later, seated among the makeshift shelters of the Paradise worksite, surrounded by workers whose language was alien to my own, I spoke with urgency, recounting my plight and pleading for help. Balasubrahmanyam said only one thing: 'This is no longer about helping you, Sheshadri – you are helping our movement.

"Everything happened quickly after that. Clad in crisp, formal attire, Balasubrahmanyam swiftly accompanied me. When we reached the private jetty and boarded the boat, I lied to the driver: 'The Country Head summoned us urgently. He insisted I bring this man along. Take us there quickly...'

"The driver hesitated and said, 'There's an event going on there. I was even instructed to return to the shore. I've been told to go only when summoned.' But I interjected with another lie: 'The Head insisted we be there for the event. He warned about being late. So let's move quickly.'

"As the driver reached for his phone, Balasubrahmanyam, without hesitation, pressed the cold barrel of a pistol to his head. The driver froze. Not another word passed between us. The boat began to move, the sea breeze swayed the Rudrabhoomi on my chest.

"When I climbed to the platform of the boat, the

silencer-equipped pistol in Balasubrahmanyam's hand shifted slightly. Moments later, the driver's lifeless body was cast into the sea, and Balasubrahmanyam secured the boat before following me.

"The reception hall was eerily empty. Faint voices emanated from the conference hall beneath the deck. It was Nijad's voice, commanding and resonant. As we peered into the hall, we saw a small gathering of about fifteen people, raptly listening. Though we caught only fragments of the conversation, Nijad's voice carried an unmistakable authority: 'That's why I brought you here. As we discussed, there are several strategies for invasion. Among them, war, money, propaganda, or the imposition of ideologies – all of these stir national and local sentiments. Not only that, they may sometimes attract international attention. Therefore, we have only two options ahead of us: the womb and the land.'

"He paused, scanning the room. Detecting hesitation, he continued, his tone sharp: 'Breed our progeny in the wombs here. Let that old strategy proceed on its own path. Meanwhile, as a practical and easier route, let's now take the land route. Whatever the cost, we must acquire as much land here as possible. That way, we alone become the rightful owners of this land.'

"A murmur of uncertainty rose from the audience. Nijad silenced it with a resolute reply: 'Whatever the cost, acquire as much land as possible. Since there is a limit to how much land individuals can own here, we've started companies and their associated land banks under various names. For each location, we've chosen names for the land banks that ignite local sentiments. We've selected individuals from the upper echelons of society and those with influence as their executives...'

"A concern arose about the source of funds and how locals might suspect them. Nijad provided an answer: 'The price we pay for the land must officially come through NRI accounts. Merchants, industrialists, and officials abroad can send foreign currency through their accounts without restrictions. We route the required money through the accounts of our own people. Undocumented amounts can be given as cash. For instance, if a cent of land costs ten lakh rupees, it's enough to record one lakh rupees in the deed, with the remaining nine lakh paid as cash.'

"When someone questioned the risk of counterfeit currency being discovered, Nijad's response revealed a startling secret: 'We possess the same machines used to print Indian currency. The same paper, the same ink. Even the numbering and bundling are identical. Not even FND machines can detect a difference – it's flawless.'

"Nijad moved to his next directive: 'Given the coastal borders here, it is imperative to acquire as much land as possible along the shores. In addition to our land banks, target areas around airports, rail and bus stations, ports, and isolated islands – no matter the cost.'

"After dispelling all doubts, Nijad proceeded to deliver his fourth directive: 'Our national borders here are coastal, which makes them strategically vital. Beyond our established land banks, each of you must acquire as much land as possible – around airports, near railway and bus stations, in proximity to ports, and on isolated islands – whatever the cost. Ensure that influential locals are at the forefront of these purchases. Oppositions must be handled with incentives. If someone proves unyielding, sow discord within their ranks and let them destroy each other. And if even that fails – eliminate them discreetly.''

"He paused, then smirked. 'Oh, and tomorrow, you'll read in the papers about Venkiteswaran's untimely demise. A simple man who stood in the way of our Kundannoor operation is no longer with us. A good man, gone for a better cause – ours.'

"I couldn't listen any longer. My stomach churned with rage and fear, but Balasubrahmanyam's hand on my arm steadied me. Leaning in, Balasubrahmanyam whispered: 'Stay sharp. We'll act when the moment is right.'

"We slipped away, descending to the dining hall. The sight of attendants waiting with dishes for the guests took us by surprise. The staff greeted us warmly, unaware of the storm brewing in their guests' minds.

"Seizing an opportunity, I excused myself: 'I need a smoke,' I said, holding out a hand. 'Got a lighter?'

"Once the lighter was handed over, Balasubrahmanyam casually picked up a bottle of liquor from the table and said: 'I'll step out with him.'

"Out on the deck, Balasubrahmanyam moved ahead purposefully, with me following close behind. Despite his engineering expertise, it took him some effort to locate and open the ship's fuel tank. He poured the liquor over it and, with a calm efficiency, struck the lighter. As he tossed it in, flames roared to life.

"As flames engulfed the ship, Balasubrahmanyam untied the boat and shouted, 'Get in – quick!'

"I didn't look back. As the flames consumed the ship, our boat sped into the distance. A figure on the blazing deck caught sight of us and shouted: 'It's that Swami!', 'Capture him!', 'Get a boat – now!' But I was unmoved by the chaos. Amidst the distant shouts, the tumult on my chest – the Rudrabhoomi – roared louder than the ship.

"When we reached the shore, Balasubrahmanyam turned to me, his voice calm but final: 'This is it for me. You won't see me here again.' Then, without another word, he melted into the darkness.

"I walked straight to the sanctuary of Bhuvaneswari's temple. I was certain they wouldn't step inside. But if I went outside and those waiting outside found me, they would kill me – and more cruelly than they had killed Venkiteswaran. I sat there, silence enveloping me, and muttered: 'There's no-one here… All this land – I bought it for someone else. I drove out the villagers. Now, this street is empty. Not a soul walks it anymore. Not even one.'

"I paused, my shoulders slumping under the weight of regret. Then, a realisation struck me: 'This temple – it used to be alive, bustling with people. Now, I wait for someone to walk in.'

"A shadow of despair fell over me before I spoke to myself again, my heart heavy with remorse: 'My friend, I sold my land. No... I betrayed it. That was a sin, and sins carry a price – death. I was afraid to accept that punishment. I now realise. that fear has consumed me.'

After a long silence, Sheshadri raised the metal piece around his neck said with quiet pride: "Fear is death. Rudrabhoomi is the sanctuary for the dead. My Rudrabhoomi is no longer in this land – it is within me. And here, in this emptiness, for whom is a crematorium needed?"

Clasping the metal piece with both hands, Sheshadri pressed it to his eyes with great reverence. Then, he began to rise slowly. To my astonishment, the stone serpent idols beneath the sacred fig tree seemed to rise with him.

bull man

There was once a cattle-driver named Mohammed, though everyone knew him by his full name: 'Kannoli' Mohammed.

One fine day...

With the anklets on his legs jingling in a peculiar rhythm, Kannoli Mohammed began to tell a story. Vasu, the man who had come to show the way, took a cautious step back, offering a warning:

"Be careful, sir. When he tells his own story, he becomes... unpredictable. It's a sign that he's on the verge of turning violent."

I pretended not to hear him.

I was certain Mohammed wouldn't turn violent – and even if he did, he wouldn't harm me. He liked me too much for that. Mohammed had once told me:

"*Maashe*, there's only one person I like more than myself – and that's you."

When Mohammed started his story again, picking up from where he'd left off, Vasu shrank back in fear and withdrew.

Then, it was just me and Mohammed.

"Mohammed..."

I gently touched his shoulder and asked, "Mohammed, what happened to you?"

I wasn't sure if he recognised me. But he turned to look at me. A sharp, piercing gaze. Against the backdrop of his unkempt beard, tangled long hair, and wild appearance – that gaze was terrifying.

I flinched. But I concealed my unease and asked again, calmly: "Mohammed, don't you recognise me? It's me."

The intensity in Mohammed's eyes gradually faded. He glanced down at his anklets, then at the chains wrapped around his legs.

That was when I noticed it – the sores from the anklets had begun to break open. His legs bore wounds and grime. His knees, hidden by a tattered *mundu*, were frayed and torn. His body showed marks of beatings, and his arms and legs were emaciated.

Could such drastic changes come from a short period of illness? Mohammed had once been handsome and gentle.

When I first arrived in Malappuram after a transfer, it was Mohammed who greeted me. I had been searching for Pokkar Haji's house. As I was asking around, someone opened the car door, climbed into the front seat, and offered to guide me.

"Come, Maashe. I'll show you the way."

That was the beginning of our bond. For the next ten years, Mohammed became my shadow. Soon, he became my trusted aide in the outhouse of the sprawling house of Pokkar Haji in Valiyangadi.

The recommendation of Haji, who had been a close confidant of my father, had sealed the arrangement.

"He's a good man. If he's not working, keep him with you," Haji said.

At first, I didn't know what Mohammed's job was. When I found out, I was struck by the demands it made. He worked for butchers in places like Tirur, Tanur, and Parappanangadi. Mohammed's task was to herd cattle purchased from the Vaniyamkulam market and deliver them, on foot, to the butchers. It was a heavy-duty job, one that earned him the nickname Kannoli Mohammed. Without the prefix 'kannoli', which meant cattle-driver, no-one would recognise him.

Despite having no formal education, Mohammed possessed exceptional expertise in his trade. He was the only kannoli in the region capable of handling massive herds – twenty, thirty, or even forty cattle at once without losing control. Once, I had the chance to watch him in action. Mohammed expertly guided a large herd, skilfully keeping them in line as he moved them along the road, switching between the front, sides, and back.

"Maashe, you'll have to walk for two nights straight. Can you manage?" Mohammed asked me.

I agreed to go with him.

Back then, the weekly cattle market in Vaniyamkulam was held on Wednesdays. We arrived there by Tuesday evening, and by late Wednesday afternoon, we began the return journey with thirty-two cattle purchased by Mohammed's regular clients – Isaaq of Tirur, Hakeem of Tanur, and Koyakkutty of Parappanangadi. Each buyer's cattle were carefully marked for identification – ten for Tanur, sixteen for Tirur, and six for Parappanangadi.

As we set off, I felt Mohammed didn't view his task as just a routine thing. It seemed to me as though he regarded it as a sacred duty. Despite carrying a staff, not once did Mohammed strike the cattle with it.

By the time we left Vaniyamkulam and traversed the forest paths along the river to reach the old trade route at Vandithadam, it was well past midnight. Along the way, truck drivers, especially lorry drivers, kept hurling abuses at us. Whenever Mohammed heard these, he would ask me:

"Maashe, how can cattle understand the man-made traffic rules? Isn't it unfair to be angry with them for wandering into the middle of the street?"

I would reassure him with a simple, "It's alright, Mohammed."

At Vandithadam, Mohammed found a secluded spot, untied the cattle, and fed them hay and water before having his own meal. Once the cattle settled down to rest, so did Mohammed. Two hours of sleep later, we resumed our journey.

By dawn, we reached Thanneerpandal on the main road, ending the journey for the day. Mohammed told me that we could rest until evening before continuing. "By midnight, we'll pass through Perinthalmanna and Kottakkal, and reach Tirur," he said.

After letting the cattle rest, Mohammed said as though revealing a secret: "The sun is up. Don't make them walk in the heat."

Then, he explained why:

"Cattle meant for slaughter must not be made to endure the sun. They shouldn't be exhausted, hungry, or frightened, lest their meat becomes tough, loses its tenderness and taste."

He learnt that wisdom from his teacher, Kallan Khadar.

Khadar was more than a teacher to Mohammed – he was a father, mother and a god-like figure.

When Khadar discovered him under the thatched shed of Andichami at the Vaniyamkulam market, Mohammed was just eight years old, with no recollection of his family, home, or even his own name. Khadar, who hailed from Perinthalmanna, was Valluvanad's first known kannoli. He stumbled upon the boy while walking through the market at dawn.

Khadar woke the boy up and questioned him thoroughly: "Who are you? Where is your home? What is your name? Why are you here?"

The boy's answer was the same to every question: "I don't know."

Despite his reputation as a gruff and stern man, which he also felt, Khadar was moved by something about the boy. Perhaps it was the urging of the onlookers who gathered upon hearing the boy's plight, or perhaps it was a spark of compassion within him, Khadar decided to take the boy under his wing.

Khadar, unencumbered by family or commitments, welcomed the boy into his life. And that same day, the boy accompanied Khadar on a cattle-driving journey to Tirur. Upon their return, Khadar had the boy circumcised, gave him the name 'Mohammed', and declared him his son.

Khadar gradually taught Mohammed everything about the trade: tethering the cattle together, guiding them, keeping them calm during long journeys, when and where to stop, and proper feeding and watering techniques. He also imparted one essential lesson that Mohammed held onto for life:

"Every animal you drive knows it is on its way to the slaughterhouse. Treat them with utmost kindness. Never provoke or harm them."

Mohammed followed this teaching to the letter.

For years, Mohammed walked alongside Khadar, guiding cattle from Vaniyamkulam market to their destinations with quiet compassion. However, time took its toll, and Khadar grew too old to continue. He entrusted the trade and its principles to Mohammed.

Within a short span, Mohammed surpassed even Khadar's reputation. The cattle he guided never showed signs of exhaustion, and the quality and quantity of their meat were outstanding. For the butchers of Tirur, Tanur, and Parappanangadi, that became a matter of faith.

After Khadar's passing, Mohammed moved to Malappuram. He continued his work while living under the patronage of Pokkar Haji. It was during then that I first encountered him.

Despite our vastly different backgrounds, an inexplicable bond formed between us – something that transcended lifetimes. Mohammed, who lived with me, seamlessly took on various roles in my life: servant, companion, brother, and teacher. There was nothing we didn't share – no secrets left unspoken.

When the time came for us to part ways after ten years, my sadness was palpable. Mohammed, ever practical, reassured me:

"Getting a job abroad is a great blessing, Maashe. You should go." After a prolonged silence, he added with quiet conviction: "Maashe, you'll always be in my heart, just as I will be in yours. There's no need for letters between us. Besides, I'm illiterate, and I wouldn't want anyone else reading your words."

It was an unusual restriction, but those were moments when I felt a deep admiration for Mohammed.

I honoured his wish for five years. Upon my return to my homeland, I couldn't stay away for long before visiting Malappuram to see him.

However, everything had changed. Valiyangadi was unrecognisable, and Pokkar Haji's bungalow had been converted into a government office.

I looked for Mohammed, asking several people. Finally, Ali Master shared the grim news:

"He's gone completely mad. There's no-one to look after him. His wife died during childbirth. Kuttiyamu Vaidhyar, a traditional healer, has taken pity on him – tying him up in the workshop near his paddy field and providing treatment. Everything happens by Allah's will," Ali Master said, trying to console me. He sent Vasu along to guide me to the spot.

As I approached Mohammed, Ali Master's parting words echoed in my mind:

"He's unpredictable. Be careful. But don't worry though – Vasu is with you. He's the only one brave enough to approach him close."

However, Vasu had already retreated, leaving me alone. That didn't bother me, though. No matter how deranged Mohammed's mental state, I knew he would recognise me.

I gently touched his hand, hoping to attract his attention.

"Mohammed," I asked softly, "shall I take you with me? Let's go see a doctor."

For a moment, he glanced at me, his gaze shifting briefly before returning to its distant stare. Sensing an opportunity, I moved closer and urged him: "Say something, Mohammed. If you don't, I'll leave right now."

His eyes welled up with tears and his lips quivered as he finally spoke: "Maashe, I saw you… at least now. That's enough…"

After a pause, he stared deep into my eyes and asked with a trembling voice: "Am I mad, Maashe?"

My voice cracked as I reassured him: "There's nothing wrong with you, Mohammed. Who did this to you? Why did they do this?"

For a while, there was silence. Then, as though a dam had burst, he began to cry uncontrollably. He shared his story.

Mohammed's life had been filled with unbearable loneliness after I left for abroad. The solitude suffocated him, and the longing for companionship grew unbearable.

At the insistence of Pokkar Haji, Mohammed married Khadija, the daughter of Mukri Mustafa, who had drowned. She brought peace into his life, and together they were given a small house to live in, built on excess government land. Their marriage was blissful until tragedy struck, and a devastating pattern emerged.

A year after their marriage, Khadija gave birth to a stillborn child. The same heartbreak repeated itself a year later. When Khadija conceived for the third time, Mohammed prayed fervently for the baby's survival. But fate was unrelenting, and the third child was also stillborn.

Khadija was devastated. Days of despair stretched into months, and then years. When Khadija became pregnant again, Mohammed dared to home.

One day, as Mohammed returned home after bringing cattle from Vaniyamkulam and leaving them at the slaughterhouse, Khadija, who was heavily pregnant, began to wail uncontrollably. She was trembling and cried out:

"Mohammed, you don't understand your sin? Every week you send so many innocent lives to their death! You are the pimp of death itself. This will be your punishment. All your children will be stillborn."

Khadija's words cut deep, leaving Mohammed shaken. For the first time, he saw himself through her eyes – a man complicit in the slaughter of innocent animals. The faces of the cattle he had led to their deaths haunted him, their suffering a weight he could no longer bear.

That night, he lay awake for a long time, restless. In the middle of his sleeplessness, he had a dream in which a formless figure appeared and told him:

"Your desire for repentance has been understood. There is atonement for your sins."

He woke up feeling deeply unsettled. Khadija's prophetic words and the formless one's directions in his dream clouded his thoughts like an enigma. But it didn't last long. By the time it was time for him to leave for the market in Vaniyamkulam, Mohammed had forgotten all that.

That day, the market was almost deserted because of a local *bandh*. Hakim from Tanur was the only buyer present, and he had to settle for four emaciated cattle. Mohammed tried his best to avoid making a trip for just four cattle, but Hakim insisted he had no more: "There are no other cattle left to be slaughtered," he said.

As they travelled from Vaniyamkulam via Idakkad, by the riverbank, it was nighttime. They walked for a long time – it seemed the cattle knew the route they had taken. The night sky was beautiful, with a bright moon and stars casting their soft light over the landscape. Moonlight petals drifted down from the cloudless sky, they floated on riverbanks and smiled. As they walked, the animals suddenly stopped, turned to him, and began to moo in unison. Mohammed felt a shiver run down his spine. Were they crying? The sound was haunting, a plea that seemed to come from the very depths of their souls:

"We haven't lived long enough. Don't send us to die!"

In that moment, the memories came flooding back – Khadija's words, the dream, and the weight of his past actions. Mohammed knew it was time for atonement. On the riverbank, he knelt, overcome with emotion, and begged the cattle:

"Forgive me, forgive me..."

He untied the ropes binding the oxen and cattle, removed the cattle nose ropes and released them. They walked around him in a rhythmic way before dashing towards the bushes in a straight line. Before disappearing into the woods, they turned to look at Mohammed one last time. Their eyes shone brighter than the moonlight.

In that instant, Mohammed felt an unparalleled sense of bliss. Delicate, chilled moonlight petals rained down upon him, enveloping him in their gentle touch. Amidst the ethereal moonlight flowers, Mohammed lay serene, a fragile bloom on the sand.

When he woke up, he was startled to see a group of people around him beneath the hot sun. Familiar faces looked down at him with concern.

"Did the cattle break free? Should we surround the forest and round them up?"

Mohammed did not respond. He walked through the crowd as if in a dream.

When he reached home, he announced his decision to his wife: "I will no longer be a cattle-driver."

Hakim, who assumed Mohammed had been struck by

bad luck, didn't press him for details. Trusting Mohammed completely, Hakim settled for half the compensation.

The next week, Mohammed didn't go to the market. He was running a fever. His clients thought that he was staying home to care for his pregnant wife.

Later, when he was about to leave to buy medicine, something strange happened. A cat, which ran around the house crying loudly, blocked Mohammed's path and growled: "Can you remove the thorn stuck on my hind leg?"

Mohammed instantly understood what the cat was saying. He removed a big thorn lodged in its paw and the cat purred in gratitude.

As he stepped outside, a cow tied near the paddy field bleated pitifully: "Would someone untie me? The boundary of the field is full of lush grass. Let me eat, I'm starving."

Mohammed untied the cow. The joy it showed was a sight to behold.

Mohammed was about to take a shortcut through Kuttappi's small plot to reach his destination faster. But the dog tied in the house veranda growled menacingly: "I am the watch dog of this place. It's not right for you to trespass. If you cross, I will be forced to attack."

Mohammed understood the dog's warning, turned and took the longer route through the alley towards the market. As he walked, a strange fear crept over him. It was a bewildering realisation – could it be possible that he truly understood the language of animals?

He had to pass the mosque junction to turn towards the marketplace. As he neared the mosque, Mohammed paused and prayed: "God, are you granting me divine powers, or is this merely a hallucination?"

Before he could finish his prayer, he heard the bells on cattle being herded.

He turned around and saw cattle being brought from Vaniyamkulam, driven by someone new.

As they approached, the cattle cried out, panting in exhaustion: "Save us, save us! Can't you see that we are being led to our deaths? We yearn to live on. Save us... Please save us..."

For a moment, Mohammed felt an overwhelming urge to intervene and set them free. But then he regained control. It was the mosque compound – people would gather, and there would be consequences.

The sound of bells faded into the distance as the herd was led away. But a young bull broke free from the herd and stood defiantly on the road. It locked eyes with Mohammed and shouted: "Mohammed, you are forgetting your mission..."

Before it could finish, the stick landed on its back.

Unable to bear the sight, Mohammed closed his eyes. A feeling of guilt, like he had committed an unforgivable crime, overwhelmed him and drained him of all strength.

Nothing else came to Mohammed's mind after that incident, and he didn't bother to visit the *vaidyan*.

When he returned home, Khadija was writhing in labour pain. Although the door to the inner room was closed, the agitation of Kalikutty, the country midwife who had come to help, was evident from outside.

Overwhelmed, Mohammed felt an intense urge to pray. His prayers were answered almost immediately. A baby's cry pierced the air, a sound so breathtakingly beautiful it captivated Mohammed's heart. The rhythmic melody of the baby's wails, oscillating between high and low tones, was hypnotic. Entranced, Mohammed stood frozen, drinking in the sound, yet craving more.

Mohammed's longing to see his child's face became unbearable. He pushed aside his hesitation and tried to enter the inner room, disregarding the closed door. Kalikutty's startled cry halted him momentarily.

As he rushed inside, a heartbreaking scene unfolded before him. Khadija lay pale and lifeless on the delivery bed, her body drained of blood, her frame trembling violently. Beside her, the baby lay motionless.

"The baby is gone," Kalikutty whispered, her voice barely audible.

But before she could finish speaking, Khadija's lips quivered, and a faint, ethereal voice emerged, as if from a realm beyond the living: "Mohammed, you have erred. You failed in your sacred duty. This is your punishment."

Mohammed couldn't contain his emotions. Anger and regret surged within him, and he shouted back: "No! I haven't done it since. The moment I realised my mistake, I stopped. I don't harm animals anymore. I no longer guide them to their deaths."

Khadija's lips trembled again, her voice soft but resolute: "To commit a sin is one thing, but to stand idly and witness others sins without intervening them is equally wrong."

Mohammed was at a loss for words. It was as if his voice had been trapped in his throat. Mohammed's mind was filled with blurred visions of the cattle for slaughter he had encountered at the mosque junction. Among them was the restless young bull's anguished cry: "Mohammed, you are forgetting your sacred duty."

Suddenly, an overwhelming fear gripped Mohammed, paralysing him completely. He stood frozen – he was not sure for how long. When he finally opened his eyes, he saw Kalikutty covering the lifeless faces of Khadija and the baby on the bed with a white cloth.

After that, Mohammed couldn't clearly recall what happened. All he could remember was the constant echo of the voice of the formless, the sight of the young bull shouting at him from the road, and the haunting faces of Khadija and the baby. There was no room in his mind for anything else.

Still, a few events stood out clearly in his memory. One was the incident at Isaq's butcher shed, where he stealthily went and set free four calves meant for slaughter. The chaos that ensued as the cattle had bolted in every direction – Mohammed didn't even wish to recall that now. Another incident where he intercepted a group taking cattle to the slaughterhouse from Vaniyamkulam and released them by the riverbank.

By then, not just the butchers, but even the villagers had turned against him. They too had complaints about him. Mohammed would talk to the sheep and cattle, tied in sheds. If he got the chance, he would release the animals tethered in the fields, the plots, and even the stables and pens. The villagers were fearful that Mohammed, with no place to stay after the government had torn down his house on the excess government land, could return at any moment. In short, Mohammed had become a nuisance to the locals.

The wedding of Sadirikoya's daughter took place amidst that tense time. On the eve of the wedding, Mohammed, lying on the culvert along the roadside, heard a loud cry: "Save me, please… someone save me..."

The sound, laden with sorrow, stirred memories of grief within him. Recognising the voice as coming from Sadirikoya's house, Mohammed rushed towards it. As he entered the backyard, he was horrified by what he saw – a terrified goat calf trembled under the butcher knife of Musa, crying out for its life. The goat calf had the face of his baby that lay close to Khadija on the delivery bed.

Everything happened in a blur after that. Mohammed couldn't recall whether he had hacked Musa down or pushed him aside. By the time the villagers arrived and restrained him, the goat calf was held tightly to Mohammed's chest.

It was known that Kuttiyamu Vaidyar was the one who tied Mohammed to the banyan tree – Vasu was with him.

For a moment, Mohammed stood still, as if a torrential stream had suddenly stopped. Then he broke down, his emotions overflowing like a storm. His voice trembled as he asked: "Am I mad, Maashe?"

I was speechless, but my hands instinctively reached out. As I began to untie the ropes binding Mohammed's legs, a chorus of outrage erupted from behind.

"What are you doing, Maashe? Are you planning to unleash this lunatic?"

Ali Master, Vasu, and a few other villagers, their faces filled with rage, rushed forward.

"Thank God we came here to check if you were unhurt, Maashe. Who knows what might have happened?"

When Mohammed saw the angry expressions on the villagers' faces, I noticed a sudden change in him. And then, everything happened very rapidly.

Shaking the chains on his legs, Mohammed dug his heels into the ground and thrust his hands forward onto the ground, crouched like a wild bull ready to charge and let out a fierce bellow.

The shock on the villagers' faces was evident – I saw it clearly. At that moment, Mohammed and I exchanged glances, and in perfect harmony, we stared back at their frightened faces. In unison, we began narrating a tale, speaking in the same tone: "Once upon a time, there was a cattle-driver. And there was also a teacher..."

moonlight at noon

From the edge of the sky, night swooped down like a rogue vulture, flapping its dark wings. In mere moments, it perched atop the lamppost at the centre of the village, only to unfurl its shadowy wings further, engulfing the entire village in darkness. Captain Prakash Menon watched it unfold with slight embarrassment.

Even then, his left hand continued to rub his face, as if searching for the lingering marks of spit that might still remain. Standing in front of the makeshift tent, with a glass of rum in one hand and a smouldering cigarette in the other, he stared into the thickening darkness of the night. The thought struck him suddenly – the village seemed like a submissive slave waiting for his command. In that moment, did those dried-up spit stains matter any longer?

Such was the intoxicating high of victory that coursed through the Captain.

The mission was complete. All that remained was the order to return. It could arrive at any moment.

Once that happened... a wave of relief swept over him. Annual leave awaited him. He could finally step away from this grim environment for a while. He could go home and see his mother. It had been weeks since he'd heard about how she was doing.

The last letter had arrived a month and a half ago, just as Operation Storm was about to begin. As usual, among the village updates, Indu had written: "*Etta*, *Amma* is having chest pains occasionally. Whenever I push to take her to the doctor, she insists, "Let my Prakashan come.""

Poor little sister. Even though she'd grown up, she still retained that childlike innocence. When it came to their mother, could she really manage on her own? As soon as he got back to the unit, he planned to take leave. Not a single day should be wasted.

But would that be possible? Would they permit him to leave without partaking in the victory celebrations? The celebrations must have already begun. Even Commander Dinesh Rana, usually stingy with kind words, would have taken the lead this time.

"Boys, this is a day of good fortune. Let's celebrate today!"

True enough.

This was indeed a victory worthy of celebration – no doubt about it. As the Commander had predicted, their success was due to luck.

"You're not just brave, you're lucky too.

That's why you must lead," was the rationale behind the decision. The directive from Military Intelligence arrived quickly, wrapped in secrecy.

"Gurmeet Singh crossed the border with six terrorists trained in an enemy state. It is suspected that they have gone to his native village, Satpalganch."

Satpalganch lay just eighty kilometres from the Operation Storm base, close to the border. Within moments, comprehensive details about the village were compiled: a settlement of about one square kilometre in perimeter, with 132 houses and a population of around a thousand. The demographics included 407 men, 420 women, and 171 children. While terrorists had used it as a temporary hideout, the villagers were generally innocent. There were no signs of defensive preparations, making the search relatively straightforward. Even if resistance emerged, fewer than a hundred soldiers would be sufficient to handle it.

"You may choose any strategy you like."

The Commander granted him complete freedom.

What followed was swift. As they were being sent off, the Commander gave him a warning, almost like a reminder: "Gurmeet is a hardened terrorist. There's a ten-lakh bounty on his head." Yet not a flicker of hesitation crossed his mind.

As they approached the village, the final shape of the action plan was decided on. First, tents were set up on the village outskirts. Then, step by step, the search strategies were implemented. The three pathways connecting the village to the outside world were swiftly blocked and secured, effectively sealing off the village.

Instead of beginning the house-to-house search simultaneously from two sides, they employed RS tactics: – continuous, thorough sweeps starting from one end, with intervals of three to four hours between rounds. A strict warning had been issued that no-one was to leave their homes under any circumstances, leaving the villagers visibly distressed.

The words of Colonel Hamilton were clear in his mind: "It is more desirable to capture the enemy alive than to neutralise them."

Hence, the search was conducted with minimal aggression – calm and measured. The war strategies he learned from his Stanford class were ingrained in his mind like sacred texts: "Imagine the battlefield as a fight for survival and consider the opponent as someone to be subdued. Exercise maximum vigilance."

Perhaps that's why, despite the repeated, prolonged sweeps, there was no impatience or fatigue.

It was during the third round of searches that they captured the first terrorist they were looking for. There wasn't much resistance. Surrounded by weapons from all directions, he surrendered. Two more were captured during the fourth and fifth rounds. That left four more. The search continued.

By the seventh round, three more were found. That made six in total. Yet one person was still missing – Gurmeet Singh himself. While the search pressed on, those who had been captured were interrogated using various methods. Their consistent response was that Gurmeet hadn't entered the village at all.

Then who was the seventh? And where had he gone?

"There's no such person. Only six of us crossed the border," was the explanation offered by the detainees.

The unit sent a message back to headquarters. The response came swiftly: "If you're certain, the search can be called off. However, reports identify the seventh as Gurmeet Singh. Capturing him would be a major success."

It served as a spark of motivation. The detainees were tortured in the 'best' possible way. Five of them remained silent, but the sixth finally gave in: "There's a granary beneath Gurmeet's house," he said.

Gurmeet's home was the largest in the village. Within moments, all our forces converged there. Seeing the commotion, Gurmeet's elderly mother spoke up in frustration, her voice tinged with irritation: "How many times are you going to search this house? It's just me and my grown-up daughter here."

Her protests fell on deaf ears as the soldiers methodically searched the house. Room after room was cleared, until they came upon one that was locked. When they tried to open it, the old woman hesitated before saying: "My daughter is in there, changing clothes."

But there was no time to wait. The door was forced open with a rifle-butt blow. For a fleeting moment, the Captain stood frozen.

Standing before them was a beautiful young woman, with sculpted curves, her body exposed almost completely. Even in that tearing hurry, he realised that she had a wheatish complexion. She turned sharply, her loose hair cascading down her back as she tried to cover herself.

"Shut the door and keep away, I'm changing," she roared, and the Captain came back to his senses. He seemed to linger, his gaze fixed on her for another second – or had he stepped into the room? He couldn't be sure when a soft creaking sound. The wooden planks over the granary below began to move.

Everything happened in a blur after that. Shots rang out, though no-one could say how many. At last, Gurmeet Singh's lifeless body, drained of blood with numerous bullet wounds, was dragged out of the hidden compartment beneath the granary. His elderly mother collapsed to the ground, unconscious.

The young woman screamed hysterically, seeming to forget her half-naked state. If not for the firm hands of the soldiers restraining her, she might have done something reckless.

Even then, she managed one final act of defiance – she spat on Captain Prakash Menon's face.

The Captain's hands moved to his face almost involuntarily, rubbing as if to erase something. Were the traces of that spit still lingering there? He had taken blows to the face in a boxing ring before. His face had been bruised during military training. He had even been wounded in battle. But this was the first time someone had spat on his face – and that too, a woman.

Even as he stood alone between the wings of darkness in the night, an inescapable feeling of terrible disgrace began to wrap him in like an unwanted shroud.

He couldn't endure it much longer. To shake off the humiliation, he downed the rum in his glass in a single gulp. As the fiery warmth coursed down his throat, spreading through his body, Captain Menon realised it wasn't bringing him relief. If anything, it deepened his unease.

He flicked away his smouldering cigarette, reached down for the bottle on the ground, and poured himself another glass. This time, no water – just pure rum.

One single gulp, no water. And another. Yet the gnawing discomfort of that insult refused to leave him. It clung to him, sharp and stubborn.

She had spat on him in front of his own men. A woman dared to do that to him. Such audacity couldn't be forgiven.

Captain Prakash Menon clenched his jaw. She must know who I am. She must understand I am a man.

He opened a fresh bottle and lit another cigarette. As his glass was filled and emptied repeatedly, his mind became a hazy swirl of smoke and unsettling thoughts. And through that haze, that image began to emerge again – clear, vivid, unshakeable. Her wheat-coloured skin, those delicate curves, the cascade of dishevelled hair, and beneath it all, the fullness of her figure. And then – the spit.

The thought of it burned through him like an ember refusing to die. Captain Menon tried to think of anything else to drown out that image. But nothing worked.

The smoke enveloped everything and within it, only that sight remained.

Captain Prakash Menon wasn't certain what had happened next. He didn't recall the jeep's engine starting, nor did he notice it racing through the dark and deserted lanes of the village. It was only when the jeep came to a screeching halt in front of Gurmeet's house that he snapped out of his daze.

Even though he knew no-one else was around during that time of the night, he scanned his surroundings cautiously. Nothing. Not the slightest sound or movement disturbed the silence. The village lay still, crushed beneath the oppressive wings of the night.

Jumping down from the jeep, the Captain began walking toward the house. He paused as he reached the outer door. Was there a faint light flickering inside? Or perhaps the low, muffled sound of grieving?

He didn't wait to confirm. With one powerful kick, he broke open the door and barged in – only to be stopped in his tracks by the sight before him.

Illuminated by the dim glow of a dying oil lamp, a still human figure lay wrapped in a white cloth on the floor. Beside it knelt a young woman, her body wracked with sobs as she leaned over the lifeless form.

Startled by the noise, the woman turned around sharply and froze for a moment as her eyes met the Captain's. Then, just as suddenly, she became nervous. The same lips that had spat at him quivered helplessly, her voice breaking as she cried: "Mother… my mother…"

The words pierced through Captain Prakash Menon. The haze of intoxication that had gripped him evaporated in an instant.

The young woman rose to her feet in desperation, reaching out with a trembling hand, clutching his arm like a lifeline, pointing to the lifeless form on the floor and whimpering, "Mother… my mother…"

For Captain Prakash Menon, the last remnants of the intoxicating haze vanished entirely.

A sudden clarity washed over him and he became Prakashan.

A vision from his own life flashed before him. In the central hall of their ancestral home in Vadakkepattu, his mother, Ammukkuttiyamma, lay still, wrapped in a pristine *kodi*. Beside her, his little sister Indu, pointing at their mother and crying out in a trembling voice, "Amma… Etta… Amma…"

Unconsciously, his arms moved forward, pulling the sobbing woman in front of him into his embrace. Despite every effort to suppress it, something deep within him broke free – an uncontrollable surge of emotion. And from the depths of his soul, it spilled out in a choked whisper, "My child... Indu..."

Hearing this strange, unfamiliar language amidst her sobs, the woman lifted her head, confused and tearful.

Outside, atop the village lamppost, the night like a rogue vulture folded its dark wings and prepared to take flight. Far on the horizon, at the edge of the sky, the faint hue of moonlight had just begun to spread.

goddess of vengeance

Durgamma was stunned. How could the sea waves feel so warm on this chilly morning? She felt the warmth of Unni burying his face in her cupped hands – a sensation she could never forget.

As she scooped water from the sea and sprinkled it over her head for purification, it felt like Unni's mischievous hands brushing against her hair and face.

Durgamma couldn't hold back her tears.

"My child... How did it come to this?" If he had a sibling or an offspring like people of his age group, perhaps she wouldn't have been forced to perform these rituals, a duty typically fulfilled by children for their elderly parents.

"Mother, shouldn't my soul attain salvation? Shouldn't there be a *bali*[4] for me?"

Unni had appeared in her dreams repeatedly after his death, asking the same question. Who did Unni have other than her to perform these rites for him? In one of those dreams, she had shared her concerns with him. His response had been immediate:

"Mother, I'm sure you will be enough. I would love it if you did the *bali* yourself."

That was when she consulted the priest.

Upon hearing her request, he had refused:

---

4. A Hindu ritual for the dead

"Mothers do not offer *bali* for their children – since it is a case of unnatural death, I can perform an exorcism instead."

When she relayed the priest's verdict to Unni, he smiled and said:

"Mother, why do we need a third person between us? I will gladly accept whatever you give me."

He paused, then added: "But Mother, it's not just me. Don't you think you should perform rites for four others too? Who will do it for them?"

His words shocked her. Could the dead read truly the minds of the living? Unni was right – she had been thinking of offering *bali* for four other souls as well. In a way, it seemed Unni had also wanted that.

Durgamma recalled the moment Unni had screamed '*Amma*!' as his life slipped away in the lockup. She had collapsed on the veranda of her rented house, where she had dozed off for a few minutes while waiting for her son. She regained consciousness at the sound of Unni's desperate cry, and saw him standing beneath the ten-armed image of Durga Devi on the wall.

"*Amma*, they killed me... Don't cry. Aren't you Durga? Would Durga weep? Durga's role, as described in the Durgaashtakam, is to mete out justice and guide souls to salvation. That's what you must do, *Amma*."

Unni, who had once seemed naive and slow, spoke with remarkable clarity and wisdom after his passing. His arguments were logical, and his words were convincing.

Durgamma reached the beach before sunrise. She had arranged the materials for the ritual the previous day. Her father used to perform these rituals for her great-grandfather. Back then, she wasn't just an observer – she used to assist the priest. Those memories gave her the strength to do what was required.

The beach was deserted – or was it simply too dark to see anyone? Durgamma didn't care. At the ritual site, she arranged five banana leaves on the shore. Over each leaf, she placed the offerings: rice, sesame seeds, kusa grass, flowers, and rice balls moulded for the rites. Then she took a purifying dip in the sea and returned, knelt before the leaves with her head bowed low.

On her finger was the sacred ring called *pavithram* made of *kusa* grass. She gathered seven blades of *kusa*, braided them together and invoked the spirits for whom the offerings were intended. She laid the *kusa* grass atop the rice ball on each leaf in a south-north direction.

As she pondered who should be first, Unni's voice whispered in her ears, "I can wait till the end, *Amma*. Isn't that how it should be?"

Durgamma accepted his wishes. If so, who among the other four should go first?

At that moment, a cry pierced the silence. It was the desperate wail of a ten-year-old boy echoing from the depths of a well.

Earlier, his voice had a mocking tone. Durgamma remembered.

The boy had teased her on the school grounds while retrieving a ball that fell near her.

"Ammachi, are you here to study? Or...?"

Before he could finish his question, someone pushed him into the well.

The next morning, a neighbour, Vasu, had come with the newspaper and remarked: "Durgamma, the gods are just. One of the policemen who killed your son lost his own child in an accident yesterday. The boy fell into the school's well."

Durgamma hadn't felt any guilt upon hearing that. It had taken her three days to find the boy, the cop's son, and his school. She waited four hours over two days, hiding near the well until the boy wandered into her sight. In her haste, she forgot to ask his name.

Invoking the face of the unknown child, she performed the rites. She laid the first *kusa* grass over the rice ball and offered it water. After chanting the offering verse, she attempted to tear the banana leaf tip as part of the ritual, when two hands sprouted from her body! It startled her, but they effortlessly tore the leaf's edge.

"Child..." Durgamma whispered. "I don't know you... You are a victim of your father's sins. I didn't intend for this to happen. I was merely an instrument. May your soul find salvation alongside my son's."

She moved on to the next leaf as she kept repeating those words like a mantra and knelt. She didn't need to think about who it was for. Before that, the image of a young girl engulfed in flames filled her mind, and she heard a voice.

"Dear Chitra, turn off the TV and go to the kitchen. The rice is on the stove – lower the flame when it boils. Your father and I will return soon from the market."

Durgamma remembered watching from the shadows, waiting for the right moment to strike. The girl stood by the stove, unaware. A container of kerosene sat nearby, and without hesitation, Durgamma poured its contents over the unsuspecting child. The girl's screams were drowned out by the explosion, and Durgamma turned away, leaving behind a burning kitchen and a life reduced to ashes.

The next morning, the milkman, Maniyappan, described the incident with horror and awe.

"Oh, Durgamma, fate works so quickly now. Do you remember the inspector who killed your son? Lathi Velappan, wasn't he? His only daughter died last night in a kerosene stove explosion. Some people say it was a suicide."

The girl's name was Chitra. Durgamma thought of her as she performed the ritual. When she put the *kusha* grass on the rice ball and offered it water, two more hands sprouted from her body, joining the others. The new hands tore the edge of the leaf and set it aside with precision, as though obeying an invisible power.

Durgamma moved to the third leaf and knelt down. A gust of wind brought the image of the claimant of the third leaf to her mind: a dark-skinned, teenage boy with a folded ear. He had been sitting on the terrace parapet of the police quarters, engrossed in a book. Seeing an old woman collecting laundry nearby, he cast her a suspicious glance and tried to stare her down.

It hadn't taken much effort to push him off the railing, and the wind carried him from the third floor to the ground below.

Raju Mohandas, the boy's name, was revealed by a woman reporter on a news channel. That evening, the reporter visited Durgamma's house with a camera crew, eager to break the story.

"Ammachi, did you hear? Mohandas, one of the policemen who allegedly killed your son, lost his only son. Raju, an engineering student, fell from the police quarters terrace and died. He had ranked first in the recent entrance exam."

The reporter pressed on with questions, her excitement barely contained.

"I'm running a story on this in the last bulletin tonight. Where human justice fails, nature's justice prevails. What do you think about that? Doesn't it seem like the children of those who wronged your son are being called back by nature?"

Durgamma had said nothing. She hadn't even looked up as the camera captured something under bright lights.

A similar wind swept through when she left.

"That should be the soul of the brilliant student Raju Mohandas," she said to herself. "It should also get salvation."

With a focussed mind, Durgamma offered water to the departed soul. And, as before, two more hands emerged from her body, tore the leaf's tip, and laid it aside.

The fourth leaf carried a distinct, nauseating smell which made Durgamma very uneasy. It was the scent of people who try to kill themselves by taking poison, reminiscent of her friend

Janamma's tragic death years ago. Janamma, shamed by her pregnancy before marriage, had consumed poison.

That smell had returned recently, just before Sivan's death three months ago.

Durgamma remembered Sivan unexpectedly walking into her home, drunk and unsteady, clutching a packet. There had always been bitterness between them – Sivan was the man who had lured Unni to his death. She had watched him with quiet vigilance and perhaps he sensed it and kept away till then.

What was the purpose of his visit after all was said and done? She observed with alertness.

Even in his intoxicated state, Sivan seemed hesitant, searching for the right words. Finally, gathering his courage, Sivan began. "*Amma...*" His voice wavered. "*Amma*, your son is gone."

His drunken haze stripped away his restraint and he confessed. "My Unni... I saw those police officers kill him with my own eyes. But in court, I lied... I was afraid for my life. They gave me money..."

He paused, his breathing heavy. "If I hadn't lied, they said they'd frame me in numerous cases and lock me up for life."

He sat down, his limbs unsteady, struck his own chest and spoke in a curious rhythm. "Amma, I will be there for you, I will take Unni's place... While drinking toddy, I remembered you. I didn't eat my meal, instead got it parcelled and brought it here. Let's eat together tonight."

He opened the packet and spoke to himself. "I have eaten so much food at this place... So much food you served me... Sivan won't ever forget that. Today, I will serve you and Amma will eat..."

It didn't take long for her to realise that a stage had come when Sivan couldn't keep anything secret. This wasn't new behaviour – Sivan had always been loose-lipped after a few drinks. Sivan was Unni's only friend, and despite a few people telling her that he was taking advantage of her naive son, she allowed the friendship to grow – she thought her son should also have a friend.

Sivan frequently visited their home, sometimes arriving drunk. Once he'd had a few drinks, he'd speak freely, revealing his innermost thoughts. That didn't change at all, she realised. She used the opportunity cunningly to ferret out every information he had on the death of Unni. And he disclosed everything.

Sivan's voice seemed to carry Unni's words as if they were echoing in the air.

Unni had once shared his greatest dream with Sivan, something he had silently dreamed of for years – to give his mother a special Onam gift.

Unni had heard his mother speaking several times about the Onam gift his father had once brought her – a glittering saree adorned with a three line *kasavu* (gold border). During their first Onam after marriage, his father had gone to Balaramapuram to get a saree woven for his mother. Upon seeing it, her mother-in-law was adamant that it should be given to her own daughter, who was on the verge of divorce. His father was not one who could defy his mother's words. The saree his mother had longed for was taken from her and handed to someone else. His father had consoled her, promising that he would get her a new saree the following year.

That promise went unfulfilled, as Unni's father succumbed to a snake bite before the next Onam festival. After that, Unni's grandmother took over their household, threw out Unni's mother without giving her anything. Her ancestral family had crumbled and was incapable of helping out Durga. Her mother-in-law revelled in torturing her daughter-in-law, who hailed from a poor family. Unni's mother had lived through enough sorrow to last an entire life in a single year, she had said. She was forced to leave without anyone to support her family – she had to live like a servant in a distant relative's house. When she found the life there unbearable, she had to become a house maid.

Finally, she had managed to secure a rented home.

Though she sent Unni to school, he couldn't really learn, as he had learning disabilities. As he grew older, he didn't have the capability to work or support his family on his own. He had wanted everything but lacked the drive to follow through. For years, she fed him the food she brought from other households where she worked.

In the last five or six months before her death, there was a noticeable change in Unni. She was bedridden with fever and perhaps, that sparked the transformation. A desire to provide for her through his own efforts. Unni attributed this change to his mother's fervent prayers to Goddess Durga.

Unni's determination to realise his dream was palpable. He had worked tirelessly, starting at an auto workshop, then moving to car washing in Lorry Pettah. Six months later, he proudly shared with Sivan that he had saved two thousand rupees. One day, he confided in Sivan about his plan – to surprise his mother with a saree for Onam, just like she had always wanted. He swore Sivan to secrecy until the big reveal.

On Onam eve, Unni took Sivan to the city to find the perfect saree. They scoured several shops, but none had the exact saree his mother had described. Unni clutched his pocket, fearful of losing the money. Periodically, he'd pull out the cash to ensure it was still there.

A shopkeeper on the outskirts of town hinted that new stock from Balaramapuram would arrive later that evening, including the saree Unni sought. To pass the time, Sivan suggested catching a movie, but Unni declined, hesitant to spend a single rupee before buying the saree. Instead, Sivan proposed sitting at a nearby park.

As they sat on a bench, chatting idly, Unni repeatedly pulled out his money, gazed at it, and returned it to his pocket.

On one occasion, as he took the money out again, he felt a presence behind him. He turned around in shock.

A police officer loomed over him.

"Who are you? What are you doing here?" The officer's breath was thick with the smell of alcohol.

Unni froze in fear, but Sivan stepped in to explain. The next question caught them unawares.

"Where did you steal this from?"

Unni replied that he hadn't stolen it and that he had earned the money over the past six months from working.

"Walk to the station," the officer ordered brusquely.

The moment they stepped into the station, both were stripped and locked in a cell. Even then, Unni clutched the money tightly in his right hand.

A harsh voice shouted from the doorway, "Give me the money!"

The cruel head constable who entered the lockup first and Unni, half-dazed, pleaded, "This money is for buying a saree for my mother."

The sound of a slap rang through the air, loud and sharp. Unni collapsed to the floor, writhing in pain. Even then, he clutched the money tightly in his hand.

The other cop entered the lockup and stomped on Unni's hand while the head constable forced his right hand open and took the money. With his hand crushed, Unni cried out in agony, "This is the money I earned for my mother's saree."

The beatings continued – kicks, punches and blows. Unni fell, weakened.

As they left the lockup, the head constable asked the cop, "Should we release them after registering an FIR, or take them to court?"

The policeman leaned close to Unni's ear and shouted,

"You've got seventeen theft cases on your name... we'll let you go for now... get lost..."

Despite everything, Unni summoned unexpected courage and insisted, "This is my money for my mother's saree. I earned it. If you return it, I shall leave."

The cop and head constable exchanged looks, lifted Unni and pushed him against the wall. An Assistant Sub Inspector, upon hearing the commotion, rushed over. The head constable handed him the money, and they conferred privately.

"You will leave only with the confiscated money?" was the only thing they heard from the ASI. Sivan watched in horror as Unni was brutally crushed underfoot, writhing in agony and crying out.

Unni lay helpless under six boots. Somewhere in the chaos, he was handcuffed, his legs tied together, and a cloth shoved into his mouth.

After an eternity of torture, the cops said, "We'll present you in court tomorrow, and then we'll let you go."

Unni could barely hear them. He was groaning and moaning in pain. In a faint voice, he begged for water, but it was not there in the cell. The stench of urine emanated from the earthenware jug.

Later that night, the same trio of cops entered the lockup again, reeking of alcohol. Unni, despite his fear, asked for water. The heavily drunk cop laughed, unzipped his pants, and urinated, the sound echoing through the cell. Unni spat in revulsion and gasped.

"Sign these blank papers and get out," the ASI said, as though performing an act of kindness. Until then, Unni had been lying still, but then, he managed to plead, "This money is for my mother's saree. Return it and I'll leave."

"You will leave with the money," the officers sneered and pushed him down to the ground. They began kicking him again.

For a while, the sounds of his desperate cries echoed through the cell. Then the noises of boots stamping on the ground and the squelching of mud mixed in, growing louder. At one point, Unni's faint call, "Mother!", was heard clearly.

Finally, one of the cops muttered, "It seems he's done for. Let's take him to the hospital quickly."

The officers quickly lifted Unni, dragging him outside. The sound of a jeep starting and moving away was the last thing Sivan heard.

The next morning, the same cop-trio arrived at the lockup and told Sivan, "You and your friend had gone to a second show and were caught when he tried to pickpocket someone in the crowd. The witnesses attacked you. We arrived and took him to the hospital. You were brought here."

While Sivan was still confused, they continued, "He's dead. How can someone survive after being attacked by a mob? We have brought you here since you were alive. Get it?"

They repeated this narrative, forcing Sivan to sign numerous papers. Afterward, they took him to a liquor warehouse, initiating the formalities and proceedings.

"At the court, I gave my statement as instructed, and only then was I released," Sivan concluded.

Durgamma's heart seethed with anguish as she grasped the truth behind Sivan's slurred words. His silence that followed was oppressive. He opened a new bottle he had kept in his waist and took a swig. Without addressing anyone, he said:

"The one who's gone is gone... We need to live, right? Those who killed him for two thousand and five hundred rupees gave me two and a half lakhs... that cop Gopinathan sir, Head Constable Mohandas sir, Assistant Sub Inspector Velappan sir... to be honest, they're all gold-plated men... A mistake happened while being drunk. But that worked in my favour..."

Sivan's indifference was palpable as he added, "Anyway, what was Unni capable of? He was an idiot..."

Durgamma couldn't bear that. "Maybe he was an idiot; but he wasn't a pickpocket or thief! But you made him one in the eyes of the world. If you had spoken the truth, my child's name wouldn't be in tatters..."

Sivan's demeanour changed. The drunken remorse was replaced by cold defiance. "Enough, Amma," he threatened. "If you don't keep your mouth shut, you'll meet the same fate as him."

Sivan stopped in the middle as though remembering something, and pulled out a small vial from his pocket.

"You see this? It's poison. A single drop is enough... You are tormenting those good police officers with this case... Withdraw the cases against them... Isn't it better than taking poison? I have got nothing to fear. The police have promised to cover it up for me. They'll say you killed yourself out of grief."

Durgamma froze, grasping the true reason for Sivan's visit. But she swiftly composed herself, deciding to manipulate him. "You're right, Sivan, from now on, you are my son, like Unni," she said without any sense of guilt. "You're all I have now. I'll do as you say."

Sivan smirked like a victor and closed his eyes. Or was it because he was intoxicated? Durgamma seized the opportunity, swiftly mixing the vial's contents into Sivan's food.

"Eat, Sivan," she said calmly. "You've done so much for me. Let me serve you tonight."

Sivan ate heartily, oblivious to the poison taking root in his body. By dawn, he was found dead by the roadside, his lifeless body surrounded by the putrid stench of his own vomit.

The next morning, neighbours found Sivan's body and Durgamma looked at it with a sense of cruel satisfaction. The stench of his death had lingered like the smell that emanated from the fourth leaf.

Invoking Sivan's face and name, she offered water to the rice ball. Two additional hands sprouted from her body, tearing the leaf's tip and placing it aside.

As the ritual progressed, Durgamma felt a lingering sense of gratitude towards Sivan. He had revealed the truth about Unni's final moments and named the men responsible. Without him, she would never have known her son's killers, Unni's last moments and the depth of their crimes.

Finally, Durgamma knelt before the fifth leaf, her heart heavy with sorrow. That was for her son – her own Unni.

"This is for my son, Unni," she whispered to herself. "A son raised by an orphan mother, without a father's protection. A son who grew up on leftover food only to face insults. A beloved son who tried to fulfil the wishes of his mother and called for her as he was being murdered. Dear son, that mother is offering this heartfelt *bali* for you, though she is forbidden to do it."

As she invoked Unni's face and put the *kusha* grass on the rice ball, Durgamma's mind drifted back twenty-nine years to a stormy monsoon night. In the dimly lit delivery room, a midwife placed in her hands the newborn son she had delivered... When she offered water over the grass, she felt like dripping honey and a sweet flag into the tiny lips of her infant son.

The ritual was complete; Durgamma extended her hands to tear the edge of the leaf. But this time, something remarkable happened. The eight hands that had sprouted earlier kept back respectfully. Durgamma herself tore the leaf's tip, severing Unni's ties to this world.

As she finished, an inexplicable sense of peace washed over her. Her son's soul had finally found salvation, she thought.

But her journey was not yet over. She had one final task left – to decide her own fate.

As the last leaf was laid aside, Durgamma found herself in a dilemma. The Durgashtakam teaches that one must decide on the consequences of their own karma, and it was time for her to decide. Four deaths – that of three children and Sivan- weighed heavily on her mind. The depth of a well, the heat of a fire, the impact of a fall, and the potency of poison. Which of these paths should she choose for herself?

There was no need for deep contemplation. The answer unfolded before her as if the universe itself had decreed it. Durgamma gathered the remaining ritual offerings, taking all the plantain leaves together. Then, with resolute steps, she walked into the sea for ritual immersion.

It was then that she noticed for the first time – her body now bore ten arms! But Durgamma was neither shocked nor afraid. She also had no difficulty in realising why the water felt lukewarm though it was a cold morning.

Because, as she waded deeper into the water, her ten hands parting the waves, the warmth of Unni rubbing his face had spread not just in her cupped hands, but all her body.

beyond the canvas

Long, long ago, there was a king named Muthumalanaikan. He was a powerful and illustrious ruler, but he had one weakness – beautiful women. Wherever he saw a beauty, he considered it his right to possess her. And possess them, he did.

One day, while hunting in the forest, the king got separated from his men. As he wandered alone, searching for his entourage, he stumbled upon a stream. There, he saw something extraordinary. A sight that left him spellbound – a beautiful woman, naked, bathing in the crystal-clear waters cascading from a mountain stream.

The king was so captivated by the sight that he forgot he was lost in the forest. Forgetting his purpose, companions, and surroundings, he made his way toward the stream. As he approached, he realised the woman had seen him. Her gaze met his, steady and unflinching. The king couldn't bring himself to look away.

Her hair flowed like dark storm clouds, cascading behind her. Her forehead was shaped like a crescent moon, and below it, her eyebrows arched gracefully over eyes that resembled lotus petals set upside down. Her gaze held an otherworldly radiance.

Between her luminous eyes sat a slightly curved nose, with a gleaming tip that seemed to sparkle. Between her upper lip, framed by fine hairs, and a full lower lip, was a smile that bloomed without parting. Her cheeks were full and smooth, guarded by ears that stood vigilant. Below them began the slender curve of her neck. And further below...

The king couldn't believe his eyes. At the centre of her chest, there was only one breast. Just one!

For Muthumalanaikan, who had enjoyed countless women, that was a sight that he had never encountered before. His eyes locked onto the lotus-bud-like nipple of that solitary breast, which seemed like it would overflow even when held by two hands. Try as he might, he could not look away.

Overcome by curiosity and desire, the king approached.

"Fair maiden, I am Muthumalanaikan, the ruler of this land. Who are you? I wish to know everything about you."

Her lips trembled, and words fell from them like pearls. "I am Sumaja, an *apsara* (celestial nymph). I have been wandering this earth under a divine curse."

"Who cursed you? Why? Is there any way to break this curse?" the king asked eagerly.

"I cannot reveal the secret of my curse. But yes, there is a way to break it. If I unite with a celibate man, I will be freed," she explained.

At that moment, the king felt a wave of disgust for all the women he had ever known. A longing filled his heart, wishing he had lived his life untouched by women, celibate until this moment.

Suppressing a sense of shame, he asked, "Why do you seek freedom from your curse? Couldn't you live here, as the queen of Muthumalanaikan in my palace?"

"That cannot be. I must break my curse. Until then, I am destined to wander."

"No," said the king with finality. "I desire you. Whatever this king desires, he shall have. And I have decided to take you to my palace."

"That will be impossible," she replied.

"The word 'impossible' does not exist for a king," he declared, stepping into the stream.

Despite Sumaja's repeated protests, the king moved closer to her. She stepped back in fear, her voice now a firm warning.

"Do not touch me unless you are celibate. If your touch is impure, I will turn into a stone statue."

"This king has untouchability," he replied arrogantly.

As he reached out to grasp her right wrist, she warned him again, her voice trembling but resolute.

"Stop! If your touch is impure, I will turn into a stone statue."

"This king is not impure," he insisted and seized her wrist.

The moment his hand brushed her wrist, Sumaja froze into a statue. A marble statue that came up on its own in the roaring steam.

Broken in spirit, a remorseful Muthumalanaikan never left the side of that stream again. With a heart heavy with regret, he constructed around her a beautiful stone pavilion, its intricate carvings an eloquent testament to his profound grief and undying devotion. The rest of his days were spent in meditation, his soul tethered to the silent beauty of Sumaja.

After narrating the story, Mrs Varma concluded: "They say that the Muthuvans of this region are the descendants of Muthumalanaikan." She paused briefly, then added in a mystery-filled tone: "The people here share a strange belief. If a man who has lived as celibate life all along touches the right fingertip of the statue and says, 'I have never touched a woman – not with mind nor body – I am in love with you, will you come to me tonight?' – and if his words are true, Sumaja will materialise before him. She will be freed from her curse."

Upon realising the seriousness in Mrs Varma's voice, Krishnadas, who was engrossed in the magic of her tale, burst into guffaws.

"Why are you laughing, Das?" asked Mrs Varma.

"It's not the Muthuvan legend, but the seriousness in your

voice that made me laugh. You sound like you genuinely believe this," he teased.

She replied sharply, yet with a hint of wisdom. "All truths were just beliefs or imaginations in their primal forms, weren't they?"

Krishna Das's laughter faded. Observing this, Mrs Varma quickly changed the subject.

"Do you like this place, Das?"

"Very much," he replied.

"I felt the same when I first saw it," she said. "That's why we bought this estate, even though it's deep within the forest."

Feigning urgency, she added, "We've been here for quite some time – shouldn't we leave now?"

Krishnadas shook his head. "No, you go on, Mrs Varma. I'd like to stay here a little longer."

Facing the stone idol, Krishna Das lay back on the dry rock surface. His thoughts wandered, and he silently thanked his editor. It was a good decision, he admitted, to have paved the way for him to come here. Initially, however, he'd been filled with annoyance at the abrupt assignment. He thought back to that fateful conversation:

"Das, I've got a special assignment for you," his editor had said.

When Krishna Das hesitated, the editor explained: "Our chief's close friend, Ravindra Varma of the Koyikkal Palace, is organising an exhibition of his wife's paintings at the Academy Hall next week. You should visit and cover it before the exhibition begins. A car has been arranged for you. The paintings are at their estate bungalow in Muthumala. If you leave tonight, you'll reach there by early morning."

Upon being briefed on his task, Krishna Das' first reaction was self-pity.

"Another whimsical indulgence of the wealthy wives!" he had muttered. "The master of the house runs around making money, while the mistress, with no concept of time, dabbles in art. And to praise such endeavours, there are pen-pushers like me!"

But then he consoled himself – at least it was a change. A brief reprieve from the monotonous task of churning out words in the concrete jungle.

The car was excellent, and so was the driver. Despite starting at dusk, they reached Muthumala by dawn the next day. From the main road, they had to drive another hour through a forest trail to reach the estate.

The estate was a vast private property of nearly a thousand acres nestled deep in the forest. Cardamom was the primary crop, and may be due to strict regulations, not many trees had been felled. The estate itself felt like a dense forest, with entwined trees and vines dominating the landscape. Amidst all this stood the bungalow, a structure that seemed like an artifact from a bygone era.

Upon stepping out of the car, the first person Krishnadas encountered was Muniyappan. It was hard to determine whether he was an old man or middle-aged.

"Welcome," Muniyappan greeted him warmly. "The boss informed me about your arrival. Was the journey comfortable?"

Then, without waiting for a reply, he continued, "Your room is upstairs. The paintings are kept there too."

As they climbed the stairs, Muniyappan began narrating his life story, which Krishnadas found rather tiresome.

"I used to be in state service, working as a curator at the art museum... After retiring, I moved here. I have small children to support, and my pension isn't enough. That's why I took up the curator's job here..."

When Krishnadas didn't respond, Muniyappan seemed to notice his lack of interest in his life story and changed the topic.

"First, you can have a bath, then have some coffee, and get some rest. After that, you can view the paintings."

Muniyappan had laid out an itinerary for Krishnadas, but it was disrupted. As soon as Krishnadas entered the spacious hall upstairs, he froze in place, captivated by the world of colours that unfolded before him.

"Sir, I told you – you can see them later. I will get you your coffee and then let you look at these paintings and only then can I go to town for some errands. So please hurry up and freshen up."

If not for Muniyappan's insistence, Krishnadas might have remained rooted there, gazing at the paintings.

The room assigned to him resembled a king's chamber. However, Krishnadas had no time to admire its splendour, eager instead to immerse himself in the paintings.

He quickly freshened up. By the time he was ready, a meal had been brought to his room. The food was plentiful and lavish, fit for a king!

After finishing his coffee, Muniyappan guided him back to the hall. "Sir, you will be viewing the paintings, right?" he asked.

He paused for a moment before adding, "I need to go to town for some errands. I might be a little late coming back. The workers downstairs will be around – just call them if you need anything." Almost as if he'd remembered something important, he added with pride, "Pay attention to the spacing of the paintings. That's my contribution."

Krishnadas was relieved when Muniyappan left. The pull of the paintings was so strong that he barely noticed anything else.

The hall was a vast, rectangular space, hosting around thirty paintings, each one a canvas that had never known the touch of a brush. Instead, they were the result of meticulous work with a palette knife, a technique that Krishnadas found both astonishing and puzzling. How could someone achieve such precision, such detail, with an implement typically associated with less finesse?

The interplay of colours was nothing short of miraculous, with a variety of hues that seemed to vibrate with life, each canvas a testament to the artist's mastery over her medium.

Krishnadas examined each painting carefully. Viewed from different angles, the figures and emotions in the paintings seemed to undergo amazing changes, revealing new layers. One painting, in particular, held his attention – the seventh one, titled Manmathayanam (The Journey of Cupid). As he gazed at it, a figure began to emerge from the flood of colours in it – a woman's form, like a stone statue.

He moved closer, studying it intently.

Her hair flowed like dark storm clouds, cascading behind her. Her forehead was shaped like a crescent moon, and below it, her eyebrows arched gracefully over eyes that resembled lotus petals set upside down. Her gaze held an otherworldly radiance. Between her luminous eyes sat a slightly curved nose, with a gleaming tip that seemed to sparkle. In between her upper lip, framed by fine hairs, and a full lower lip, was a smile that bloomed without parting. Her cheeks were full and smooth, guarded by ears that stood vigilant. Below them began the slender curve of her neck. And further below... On her chest, in the middle of the chest, there was a single breast! Just one!

Krishnadas's eyes were fixed on the nipple of that singular breast, full to the point where it appeared it would overflow even if cupped from both sides.

He leaned closer, unable to look away, and a thought crossed his mind – the nipple seemed to glisten. Was it leaking?

As if in a trance, he extended a finger to touch it.

"Stop!"

The voice came like a command. Startled, Krishnadas

turned around. There stood a woman, her form uncannily similar to the figure in the painting.

Quickly regaining his composure, he tried to mask his embarrassment. "You're Mrs Varma, right? I didn't expect you to be here. Do you know who I am? I'm..."

Before he could finish, her voice interrupted him, firm and resolute. "I know."

He stood there, unsure of what to say, as she continued to stare at him.

After a brief pause, she asked, "Have you seen all the paintings?"

"I have," Krishnadas replied. "They're beyond what I expected. 'Sublime' would not be an exaggeration. But..."

"But what?" she pressed.

"There's something so mysterious about them," he replied hesitantly, leaving the sentence unfinished.

Her gaze sharpened. "What do you mean?"

Krishnadas, emboldened, continued, "For instance, this painting. It reveals a figure – a woman. But there's a mystery to her form..."

"I see," she said, her tone softening. "That is a copy." "A copy? Of what?" he asked.

For the first time, Mrs Varma smiled. "Not just a copy. A copy of a copy. That is when it becomes an original work..."

Her words carried the same air of mystery as the painting itself. When Krishnadas pressed her further, she explained, "There's a stream on the estate. Near its cascade is a stone statue. This painting is a replica of that statue."

Curiosity sparked within him. "Can I see it?" he asked eagerly.

"Yes, of course," she replied. "Right now, if you'd like. But it's a bit of a walk."

"I'm ready," Krishnadas said, his interest outweighing any hesitation.

As he walked with Mrs Varma toward the stream, all he could think about was that singular, striking nipple in the painting. But when they reached the secluded valley of Muthumala, amidst the dense forest and by the flowing stream, he saw the statue standing there – solitary and serene, like a hermit in meditation. It was the figure of a woman with a single breast, carved in stone. A statue of Sumaja.

While Mrs Varma narrated the legend surrounding the statue, Krishnadas's mind wandered back to his childhood, to those distant shores of memory when he would fall asleep listening to his grandmother's stories. Stories from a time when he believed that every tale had its truth, that every mystery held its magic.

Feeling that a strange sense of peace began to envelop him, Krishnadas closed his eyes gently and whispered a silent prayer: "Time, let me only swing backward forever…"

But time did not grant him his wish. When he opened his eyes, the figure of the statue came into sharp focus once more. Standing still amidst the flowing stream, beneath the ancient stone pavilion, was Sumaja's statue – helpless and unmoving.

Krishnadas couldn't lay down with his eyes shut any longer. He sat up and tried to distract himself by looking at the beauty of the forest around him. He realised with wonderment that his gaze kept returning to the statue.

Let it be so…

As he stood there, a tender emotion stirred deep within him. A thought emerged, unbidden but clear – if what Mrs Varma says was true, how tragic was Sumaja's plight!

He wondered, did Muthumalanaykkan truly spend the rest of his days here in penance? How pitiful must have been the state of his mind?

And then another thought struck him. Could Sumaja be freed of her curse if a celibate man were to stand before her, declare his love, and ask her to come to him that night?

The realisation that he was indulging in fanciful thoughts

startled Krishnadas. Also, the desire in him to wander further in the forest. He decided it was best to return to the bungalow.

His curiosity about the statue had been satisfied – there was no reason to linger. But Krishnadas did not leave. He found himself rooted to the spot.

The journey could be a pre-destined one, he thought. Then, a realisation struck him. Perhaps it was his destiny to meet Mrs Varma, hear Sumaja's story, and free her from her curse. After all, he was a man who, until now, has never desired a woman – not with his heart nor body.

Could it be that he had been chosen for this?

Guided by an inexplicable inner urge, Krishnadas approached the stream. He entered the ancient pavilion and knelt before the stone statue. With trembling hands, he touched its right fingertip and words flowed down from his heart on their own.

"I am Krishnadas, an ordinary journalist. Until today, I have never desired a woman – not with my heart nor body. In that sense, I am a celibate. Now, having heard your story, I find myself in love with you. Sumaja, will you come to me tonight?"

Krishnadas remained there, his body and soul surrendered before the statue. He continued to pray, pouring his heart into every word.

Then, he felt it – a faint movement in the statue's fingertip. Startled, he pulled his hand back and stood up hurriedly. He looked at the statue, his heart pounding.

There was a complete change in its expression. Was there a glow in its eyes? Did its serene smile spread moonlight?

Yes, the moonlight had indeed spread.

Krishnadas suddenly became aware of his surroundings. Dense desolate forest all around him – everything felt eerily silent. Fear gripped him. He regretted letting Mrs Varma leave earlier.

How would he find his way back to the bungalow? Should

he shout for help? But even if he did, would his voice carry through to the bungalow?

Realising it wasn't good to stay there, Krishnadas turned and walked away from the stream. He had barely taken a few steps when he saw a group of people approaching, their torches made from dry coconut leaves lighting up the dark path ahead. Among the voices, he recognised Muniayappan's.

"There you are, sir! We've been looking everywhere for you."

Krishnadas didn't respond. He wasn't in a state of mind to explain. Fear and confusion weighed heavily on him. He faintly heard one of the workers joke: "These writers! Probably smoked some weed by the stream and lost track of time."

Once they reached the bungalow, Muniayappan said, "Your meal is in your room. We'll be downstairs. Just call us if you need anything."

Krishnadas had no appetite, and surprisingly, he even skipped his customary pre-sleep bath, a ritual he rarely missed. All he wanted was to sleep. He turned off the lights, lay down, and closed his eyes.

But behind his closed eyelids, the stone statue stirred to life, its fearful expression etched vividly in his mind's eye. Try as he might, Krishnadas couldn't banish the haunting image.

He got up and turned on the lights, hoping the brightness would help him sleep and war away fear.

As he lay down again, unease crept in. What if someone noticed that he'd left all the lights on? Would Mrs Varma see it and come to check on him?

Suddenly, he realised the doors and windows of his room were wide open. Panicking, Krishnadas quickly shut and bolted the doors, then closed the windows. Finally, he turned off the lights.

The bungalow was now in complete darkness. Had all of them, including the workers downstairs, retired for the night?

Krishnadas's fear only grew stronger.

Desperation crept in, and Krishnadas longed to escape into sleep. But as he lay down and closed his eyes, the statue reappeared in his mind's eye, its stone form stirring, ever so subtly, to life.

No matter how hard he tried, the image couldn't be erased. Fear crept into his heart. In desperation, Krishnadas turned to the childhood prayers his mother had taught him to ward off fear. Though he felt a hint of embarrassment, he began to mutter the familiar words. Repeating the mantra 101 times, his eyelids finally grew heavy with exhaustion...

Suddenly, it happened. A touch, unlike any he had ever experienced, sent shivers down his spine. It was sensual, otherworldly, and left him breathless. Krishnadas couldn't distinguish between fear and curiosity as he slowly, hesitantly, opened his eyes. He looked around, his gaze tentative, as if afraid of what he might see.

In the faint moonlight filtering in through the window, he saw her. The stone statue, now alive, standing in his room, moving gracefully.

Krishnadas wanted to scream, but his voice was trapped in his throat. Paralysed with fear, he lay rigid, unable to move or speak.

The statue's lips moved, and words fell from them like pearls.

"Don't be afraid. I am Sumaja. I have been waiting for you to come and free me from my curse."

As she spoke, a heady fragrance rich and intoxicating enveloped everything around him.

She extended her hand toward Krishnadas.

"Come..." she said.

Then in a sudden fluid motion, she swept her hair, which flowed down like an unfurled black cloud behind her, forward, wrapping Krishnadas within its soft scented folds.

Under the fragrant cascade of her hair, something within Krishnadas changed. His fear melted away, to his amazement.

As her crescent-shaped forehead rubbed against his, he felt reborn. When the radiance in her lotus petal eyes was poured into his own, he felt he could see everything. When the soft curve of her slightly bent nose brushed against his face, he felt intoxicated. Her delicate smile, blooming yet restrained, cast a spell on him, pulling him into a trance.

The gentle thrum of her cheeks and the alertness of her ears made him further entranced. When his lips began to sweep down her slender neck to be stopped midway, he saw that even in that breathless intoxicated state...

Straight in the middle of her chest was a single breast! It was so full that even two hands cradling it from either side couldn't hold it all. Prodded by an inner urge, he brought his lips to that nipple – he understood that it was leaking!

Whatever happened afterwards, Krishnadas didn't know.

He felt himself falling into a whirlpool of forgetfulness and wonder. He clearly saw her transform into a boat – a lovely, lovable vessel gliding over the serene surface of a moonlit lake, without injuring the small ripples in it. Krishnadas was both the lone passenger and the boatman. It moved ever so slowly over the glassy waters.

As the boat glided effortlessly across the lake, the cool breeze whispered against Krishnadas's skin, gently shutting his eyes. A deep, soothing lethargy enveloped him, and he surrendered to its blissful embrace. Time lost all meaning as he floated in this serene state, until a subtle stirring deep within him jolted him awake.

It was already dawn!

The sun shone brightly outside the sealed windows, and the birds, the wind, and the forest joined in cheerful harmony.

Had it all been a dream? Krishnadas tried to recall.

No, it wasn't a dream. The intoxicating fragrance still

lingered in the room, on the bed, and in the air. His body still hummed with the blissful lethargy.

But where was she?

And then he noticed something. The door – locked from the inside the previous night – was wide open. Who had opened it?

Panic seized Krishnadas as he sat up abruptly. He had no clothes around his waist.

Had he slept naked? But for him, his clothes had never fallen off during sleep…He looked around frantically and found his clothes crumpled and discarded in the corner of the room. He quickly wrapped it around himself and began scanning the bungalow.

He checked the bathroom, the dressing room – everywhere. But she was nowhere to be found.

Could she have gone outside?

Krishnadas hurried out of the room. As soon as he stepped outside, something else caught his attention. In the hall where the paintings were displayed, there was now a large gap. The seventh painting – that of the stone statue – was missing.

Did someone remove it?

"Muniayappan!" he shouted.

Muniayappan rushed upstairs, concern etched on his face. Krishnadas pointed to the gap, his voice laced with urgency.

"Where's the painting that was kept here?"

Muniayappan chuckled. "There was never a painting there, sir. When we arranged the paintings, we left that gap for spacing between art works. Remember when I told you to check for spacing?"

Krishnadas shook his head. "No, no. I saw it with my own eyes. The painting of the stone statue... it was here."

"Such a painting never existed, sir," Muniayappan said. "I set up all the paintings here myself."

"Impossible! But I even discussed it yesterday... Call Mrs Varma!"

"Who?" Muniayappan asked, puzzled. "You mean Sumaja Madam? She's been dead for years!"

Krishnadas froze. His voice, trembling with disbelief, became almost like a wail.

His voice, trembling with disbelief, cracked into a barely audible wail.

"Then who was the woman I saw yesterday?"

"What woman? There are no women in this forest bungalow."

Who, then, had he seen? Who had walked with him to the stream? Who had told him the story? Who had invited him to free her?

A realisation struck Krishnadas like lightning. He ran down the stairs and rushed out into the forest, running toward the stream. His heart raced as he ran through the narrow forest path leading to the stream.

The forest was eerily quiet except for the distant sound of water. His footsteps quickened, driven by a mix of urgency and dread. As he reached the stream, he stopped abruptly.

The pavilion stood empty.

The statue – the lone figure of Sumaja – was gone.

Krishnadas felt a chill crawl through his veins. He stared at the pavilion in disbelief, his breath stuck in his throat. The space where the statue had stood was now vacant, as though it had never existed.

As he fell into the waters of forgetfulness with his veins shattered by that numbness, he heard the murmur of that stream quite clearly:

"Long ago... long, long ago..."